Driven

Novels by James Sallis

The Lew Griffin Books
The Long-Legged Fly
Black Hornet
Moth
Eye of the Cricket
Bluebottle
Ghost of a Flea

Other Novels
Renderings
Death Will Have Your Eyes
Cypress Grove
Drive
Cripple Creek
Salt River
The Killer is Dying
Driven

Driven

James Sallis

Poisoned Pen Press

First Edition 2012

10 9 8 7 6 5 4 3 2 1

Library of Congress Catalog Card Number: 2011644604

ISBN: 9781464200106   Hardcover
     9781464200113   Trade Paperback
     9781464200120   Large Print
     9781615953530   eBook

Poisoned Pen Press
6962 E. First Ave., Ste. 103
Scottsdale, AZ 85251
www.poisonedpenpress.com
info@poisonedpenpress.com

Printed in the United States of America

This one is for Vicky,
in appreciation
and with great affection

They came for him just after 11:00 on a Saturday morning, two of them. It was hot going hotter; sunlight caught in the fine sheen of sweat on Elsa's forehead. A hint of movement in the side of his eye as they passed a short side street—and the first one was there. He spun, slamming his foot and the whole of his body weight against the outside of the man's right knee, and heard it give. By the time the man was down, that same foot hit his throat. He shuddered twice, trying to pull in air through the shattered windpipe, and was still. The second had come up behind by then, but Driver was down, rolling, and behind *him*, left arm clamped around his neck, right elbow locked over the wrist.

It was all over in minutes. He understood then what had delayed the second man's attack. Elsa lay against the wall of an abandoned café, blood pumping from the wound beneath her breast.

She had been trying to smile up at him as the light went out of her eyes.

In movies the guy who almost drowned shoots up out of the water and into sunlight like a porpoise, gulping at the air so long denied him, relief writ large on his face.

When Driver first surfaced, six, seven years ago, it had been like that, only in reverse. Sunlight, air, and freedom—his impulse was to dive back in. He wanted the darkness, safety, anonymity. Needed it. Didn't understand how he could live without it.

He was 26.

Now he was 32, sitting at a table on the deck of HIPPIE PLACE, around to the side, away from the street.

"They first set this place down," Felix was telling him, "it was an in-your-face beachhouse. Sand every which way you looked. Kinda didn't take in as to how the hood's full of stray cats? Cats loved it, brought them in from miles around. Biggest sandbox ever, you know? Reassessments were made at the corporate level." Hands still on the table, Felix leaned back, sleeves pulling to show the lower edge of tattoos gone colorless. No hearts, anchors, women or women's names here. Knives. A flame or two. A wolf. "Long time back. And you know how few things go the distance around here. The food's crap, but it's dependable."

Driver didn't know that much about Felix, about his background anyway. Knew he'd been in Desert Storm, a Ranger he figured, from what little Felix said. And sometime before that, a gangbanger back in good old east L.A. Some kind of bodyguard or enforcer. A lifetime of walking through doors into new lives.

They'd met on a job, where it seemed Felix was along mostly to look out for one of the other guys. That's how Desert Storm came up; Felix and his boy had been in it together. Rule is, once the job's over, you're strangers. But something had clicked. Driver and Felix stayed in touch.

And who better to hang with when you went to ground? One way or another, Felix had been off the screen all his life.

"Appreciate your help," Driver said. The coffee tasted faintly of the fish tacos that were HP's specialty.

Felix's eyes followed a pair of women being seated by the front railing. Mother and daughter? Twenty, thirty years apart, dressed alike. Same body language, same legs.

"Anything else we need to do?"

"Like?"

"Oh, like persuade whoever's on your trail what a bad idea that could turn out to be."

"These aren't the kind of people you step up and talk to."

"I wasn't planning on a conversation."

"You wouldn't be. But there's no need. I've gone invisible. They can't see me. It's over."

"Invisible, huh? That's why we're sitting back here by the dumpster and you came in with a hat sitting halfway down your nose." He sipped his own coffee, made a face. "Doesn't smell near as bad as it tastes. That *is* one cool hat, though."

The older of the women smiled at Felix. Highland Park, upper East Side, Scottsdale kind of woman. Money, class, privilege. Yet here she was smiling over at this middle-aged hardass with worn-out tats and bad hair. Something about Felix did that to people.

The younger woman glanced over to see what her companion was looking at. Then she smiled too.

"All the same to you, invisible or not, I'll keep an eye out, watch for flares." Some ways, Felix never left the desert, anymore than he left L.A. He hadn't put the weight down; he carried them around inside. "Key's where it always is. Far as I know, no one's there. Someone is, you'll need to have a conversation.—Johnny, my man."

The server had come to ask if there was anything else he could do for them. Tan, blond, kid that was probably 25, looked 18 and would keep looking it till he slammed into the hard edge of 40, 45.

"We *could* use a couple of beers. When you get time. No one's in a hurry here."

Felix watched Johnny's back as he walked off, then checked his two women again. "And you have no idea who this deadly duo was?"

"Or why they showed up. None."

"They wouldn't be carrying ID."

"Doubtful. Not that I stayed around to check."

"You're sure it was a kill."

"How they came in, had to be."

"All the ways you can kill a man, that has to be the dumbest. Too many unknowns, outcome's in the wind, you're hanging out there. So why bring it in close?"

"And why take Elsa?"

"Which they did *before* putting you down. What sense does that make?"

Johnny brought the beers. He wiped the table with a damp rag, then picked up both coffee mugs with his left hand and set the bottles down with his right.

"Nothing recent to tip this," Felix said.

Driver shook his head.

"Something from the past, then."

"It usually is."

Felix took a small sip of beer and rolled it around in his mouth before swallowing. "Excellent bloom." He looked off to the tree where a bird was giving it everything it had, as though Judgment Day or final exams were in an hour. "You think birds gargle?" Then, without looking back, "In the bathroom, cabinet under the sink. Pull all the shit out, there's a board you can pry up. Just in case it turns out you need it."

"Thanks, Felix."

"Nada. Ride light, my friend."

Felix called it his warren. Unlike most souls who aren't nailed down, once he moved on from a place, he didn't let it go, he kept it. His *you-never-know* principle, that also being his rejoinder to pretty much whatever life threw at him or anything asked of him: why he did things, the actions of others, what he thought the chances were of the sun coming up tomorrow. There were Felix apartments, nondescript houses and duck-holes, scattered all around Phoenix.

This particular cell of the warren was the southeast unit of a quadraplex cut from what had been a respectable single-family house back when what was now the central city had been cozy suburbs. Latticework along one side of the drive held fragments of dead vines. Lizards scampered on the slump-block wall behind. The key was under a brick at the base of the century plant by the two-car garage that now served as storage for tenants. Driver glanced through the window. Dozens of boxes, furniture, a potbelly stove, framed paintings, an ancient Fender speaker cabinet. Looking much as it had the last time he'd seen it, better than a year ago, though chances were good that tenants had turned over two or three times since.

Driver did a quick cockroach count—two in the tub still breathing, six visible in the kitchen and mostly dead—before unpacking. Unpacking took about as long as the cockroach check had. He'd never cared much about possessions, so it had been easy walking away from the house and all the rest. Walking away from Elsa's body had been the hard thing.

He carried utility luggage, a duffel bag, with utility clothes to match: jeans, khakis, blue dress shirts and a blazer, t-shirts, underwear, black socks, all of it common stock from Target, Sears. He put the clothes away in a bureau the color of maple syrup whose uppermost layers of laminate had worn away in stages, like riverbed rock. The roach count went up by three.

Some bird had built its now abandoned nest on the outside ledge of the bedroom window, the nest spilling through a missing chunk of screen into the space between. A tiny fragment of freckled eggshell remained.

He'd been living on coffee, air, and nerves since yesterday morning, and he'd seen a diner two streets up, Billy's or Bully's, hard to tell from the sign, where the last time he'd been through, there'd been a Mexican restaurant.

Its historic smells had come forward with it to the new ownership. As though chile and cilantro and cumin were additional pigments in the wall's blue paint. Judging by the row of counter seats, booths and gunnery windows to the kitchen, the place had in some earlier incarnation been a Big Boy's or Denny's. An old man with a fringe of dandelion white hair sat at the counter, looking as though he grew there. A waiter stood off at a safe distance, talking through the half-door into the kitchen. Young couple in the back corner booth by the emergency exit, both busily engaged with hand-held devices, iPods, cells, whatever.

Driver sat down-counter from the dandelion, who kept glancing his direction. The eggs were surprisingly good, the bacon thick-cut and rimed with the perfect amount of fat. Coffee fresh, though watery. When the cook peered through the window, Driver gave him a nod and held up his fork.

Someone had scratched the name Gabriel into the counter Formica, with the blade of a pocket knife held sideways from the look of it. Driver found himself wondering during what incarnation of the diner that had happened, about the person who had done the carving, and the story behind it—his name? A friend's or loved one's? Thinking, too, about how we all struggle to leave markers behind, signs that we were here, that we passed through. How imprints like this, and like the fanciful tags on walls and buildings and overpasses, were urban equivalents of cave paintings.

He paid up at the register, $7.28, and cut through the parking lot on the way back. Just past, he came across a block of homes, five in a row, that didn't seem to belong here, so perfectly in order—windows clear, roofs free of debris, lawns freshly barbered, a quarter-inch gap at the edge of foundations, drives and walk-ways—that he wondered if the same compulsive person owned them or saw to their upkeep. Then, crossing the street, he was back in the real world, back among shambles and make-dos.

And taking note of the car parked across from his house, a sleek Buick sedan in a neighborhood of pick-ups and make-do's, single occupant.

The other one would be out back, he figured.

Driver cut around to the wall bordering the alley. Enough stuff back here, piled up along the wall, to furnish five or six homes, parts of all of it gone missing: legs on the furniture, glass in the mirrors, cords and elements on appliances. The gate, he knew from his initial reconnaissance, was held by a chain, one he'd be able to reach through the gap but not without making noise. No problem, though, since the wall was just over six feet and through the gap he could see the other guy leaning against the side of the old garage, looking toward the house.

Driver was up, over and on him as a car passed slowly out front, momentarily taking the man's atten-tion. Manicured fingernails raked Driver's arm, ruby or bloodstone ring like a fat jelly bean on one finger. A good choke hold doesn't leave much wiggle room.

It's not just the breathing, you're clamping the carotids too, shutting down blood flow to the brain. Work on kung fu movies, you spend hours hanging out with stars and stunt men while waiting to saddle up and drive. You learn things.

Without thinking—he was on some level now where thought and action were a single seamless thing—he slammed the man's body against the side of the garage, got a drumlike thud, louder than he'd anticipated, then a series of reverberations. He slipped around behind, into the narrow channel between garage and wall.

It took all of three minutes for the other one to show. Came in carrying something in his left hand, gun, slapjack, taser. Spotted his partner and moved slowly toward him. Crouched low, Driver watched through the cracks between boards.

Left-handed then. And carrying about forty extra pounds.

Driver waited.

The man drew up close, looked around one last time. Struggled some on the squat, then dropped that left hand to the ground as he eased down.

The moment the man's eyes shifted, Driver was there, stomping hard on his hand. Still wrapped around the gun handle, fingers cracked. But the man didn't make a sound. He looked up with blank eyes, waiting to see how this was going to go.

Driver kicked him in the head.

Sirens sounded in the distance, over on McDowell or thereabouts, maybe coming this way, maybe not. Driver looked around. There hadn't been enough noise to alert neighbors, but three or four two-storeys were within view, someone could have seen and called it in. He listened again for the sirens. Closer? Much as he wanted to talk to these two, to have a conversation as Felix would put it, he couldn't take the chance.

He was up the alley and around the corner when two police cars swung onto San Jacinto.

"That's your idea of laying low?"

"So I'm out of practice."

Driver was on a throwaway. Felix was calling back from the message he'd left at the tattoo parlor on Camelback.

"One might surmise that hanging out by dumpsters isn't going to make it."

"Right. Somehow they got on to me again, and fast."

"I don't like it much, either. They found you, chances are good they know more about me than anyone should."

"Just what I'm thinking, why I'm checking in."

"You put four of their people down and they're still on empty. Whatever jones they had for you at first, it's got way stiffer now. What can I do?"

"I'll need another place to stay."

"Money?"

"That's taken care of." Old habits hadn't completely passed with the old life. He had stashes of money, ID, bank cards.

"Might want to give Maurice a call."

"Your guy who does false documents?"

"Not just documents. He does whole identities—birth certificate, military, degrees. But he's just as good at erasing them. This juncture, more invisible would be wise."

"You're right."

"Swing by The Ink Spot in an hour or two. Justin'll have everything you need. Keys, clothes. Anything else you're wanting, call me direct." Felix gave him the number. "That one's with me and always on."

"Many thanks, my friend."

"Nothing. Be cool—"

"—and care. Will do." Driver hung up.

The second call was the one he dreaded, but he knew he had to make it. Mr. Jorgenson picked up on the seventh ring. Once hello was done, he said nothing further, not when Driver told him who was calling, not when he told him how sorry he was, not when he told him they wouldn't be hearing from him again.

He and Elsa had always joked about how purely middle-America her parents were. "Toasted cheese!" one of them would say, then the other: "Sectional couch!" "Jello salad!" "Mashed potatoes!" "Lawrence Welk!"

When Driver stopped talking, there was silence on the line for a time.

"Mrs. Jorgenson and I knew from the first that we didn't have the whole story, Paul. We knew that. But our girl loved you, and you loved her, and whatever *we* felt, about the strangeness that stood behind you where it couldn't be seen, about all those things that didn't quite add up—none of that came to matter much."

Silence again before he said, "How terribly we will miss her, I can't begin to tell you."

Most anyone else, Driver thought, would be dispensing homilies now: she's in a better place, she's gone to her reward, her journey's over. He could see where so much of Elsa had come from. Her spirit, the quiet at her center, her generosity.

"But we will miss you too, Paul. We *are* your family. What is going on now, once it's done, however and whatever it is, we hope you'll come back to us. We'll be here....I have to go, son."

Driver was at America's Tacos on Seventh Avenue, misters going full, no one else out here on the patio. Mostly couples inside, beyond the windows. Just two men eating alone. One of them young, crested hair, denim shirt with sleeves ripped off, head bobbing to the piped music. The other in his fifties or sixties, staring at the wall as he ate. Lost in reverie? Or to memory?

Leaving, Driver dropped his paper plate, cup, and cell phone in the recycle container.

A young woman was bent over something that looked like a gymnast's pommel horse, bare butt in the air, eating a burger as the tattooist worked on her. Every time she took a bite, a brownish mess of grease, mayonnaise and who knows what else spurted onto the floor. Hebrew letters took form slowly on her butt. Justin's eyes kept going back and forth from that butt to the printout tacked on the wall. His Rasta hair looked like something pulled down from attic storage, first thing you'd want to do is thwack out the dust. Jeans low on hips, shirtless, nipples sporting tiny gold anchors. After watching closely a moment, Driver wondered if the young woman or anyone else realized how bad Justin's eyes were.

Those who wore their exception like a billboard were a puzzle to Driver. Given his circumstances, he'd always worked hard to appear to fit in, not be noticed. But he was with them in spirit.

The tattooist's head turned. Driver watched as his eyes worked to grab and hold the new focus.

"From the look of you, no way you're here for ink, so I'm thinking you have to be Felix's friend." He laid a hand lightly on the young woman's rump. "Right back, sweetheart." She shrugged and took another bite of the burger.

Justin kicked off the wall and rode his roller chair across the floor, fetched up at the front counter and went adroitly erect.

"Clothing, laptop, sandwich, Cracker Jacks," he said, hauling a duffel bag to the countertop. "And…" snagging these from a nail in the wall, "keys. Place is a little out of the way, off the beaten path. But cozy. Or so I hear."

"Appreciate it."

"Don't see Felix do many solids like this. Marine?"

"Something like that."

"Had to be. Back to my homework, then. Phone's in there. It's safe. Felix says call him."

The woman had finished with her burger. Justin looked at the puddle on the floor and shook his head as he settled in at his post.

Back early on, back before the house, before the job, before Paul West, he had a fascination for malls. In ways he never understood, they drew him. Bright colors, lush displays in windows, the sense and sound of all those bodies moving separately and together, music, the cries of children, friendly banter. Malls were a country in miniature. He visited them, stepped into them, as though just off the ship. As though if only he sat in them long enough, put in enough miles along those arcades and scuffed floors, ate enough food court specials, something—some understanding, some sense of belonging—might solidify around him.

It was a pull he still felt when he met Elsa—at this very mall, in fact. They came back regularly. And sitting here one day, could even be the same table, he'd spoken to her about it, wondering why he kept returning.

Elsa had looked at him in that quiet way she had. "You really don't know, do you?" Eyes went up as a pigeon took wing from the struts above their heads and sailed off toward the domed roof. Did it think that was sky? "It's homework, Paul. Anthropology. You're learning how to fake it."

And he still must be—since here he was again.

He thought back to how he'd sit and eavesdrop, matching voice and cadence to appearance, this one a business woman, this one a hands-on worker, that one a teacher, moving about the scraps of sentences he overheard till a story suggested itself, the story of their lives.

To his left now sat a couple not much older than himself, man in black jeans slick at the knee, dress shirt with tail out and sleeves rolled, woman wearing loose slacks that fell to her calf, light print blouse. The man shook his head and smiled for the fifth or sixth time.

"Well, let's see, Doris. The politicians we elected are mostly rich, members of elitist societies of one kind or another, and subject to pressure groups that have nothing to do with us and everything to do with self-preservation. The companies that process our food keep on putting in more and more additives that cause heart attacks, rampant obesity, and cancer. Meanwhile, seventy percent of American viewers last night were tuned in to find out which hunk The Bachelorette would choose once she stopped crying, wiping off her mascara and spouting homilies on camera. *There's* your great country. *That's* why I have so much hope for us."

From a table occupied by two older women he heard: "Your problem, Anne, is you have to believe. That's what comes first, belief—then everything else."

And from another: "I realized just because he's dead doesn't mean I can't still write him, so I started doing that. Sat down at the computer and before I knew it I'd filled eight pages. Told him what was going on, explained things, brought him up to date with my life."

◇◇◇

Crickets outnumbered roaches a hundred to one at the new place. He'd been sitting out back near dark when they began emerging, and soon the patio, such as it was, swarmed with them, tiny ones no larger than horseflies, others maybe a half-inch. The smallest scuttled about only to fall into cracks in the cement that must be like deep trenches for them.

Crickets and cracks went a ways toward describing the new place. Water pipes barely beneath the ground, with water coming out of the cold tap lukewarm. Any available edge—roof, foundation, window, interior wall—crumbling. A wilderness of oleanders out back, their roots no doubt well along to claiming the house's sewer lines, so that you might expect them to come whipping out of the sink drain like tentacles any day now. Meanwhile, from the sound, about a hundred dove lived back in there somewhere.

His driver on the way to the mall hadn't glanced up at the rearview mirror a single time. Odd, since most cabbies learned to keep a subtle watch. Man didn't seem to have much use for mirrors period. There was a gaping wound where the driver's side mirror used to be, and glass had gone MIA from the one on the right.

Manny had thought cabs were hysterical when he called.

"Hey, that's *funny*! Guy I never knew to so much as climb in a car anyone else was driving, now he's taking cabs."

It had been a while since they talked. Manny knew about his recent life, went unsurprised at the sudden change.

"It is what it is—whatever the fuck that's supposed to mean. You notice how that line's in every damn script for the last two years? Just hunkered down in there, like a bad spot in a potato."

Manny thanked him for calling and taking him away from the shit projects on his desk.

"You hear that? Write this crap long enough, you can't think anymore, just plug in a few familiar words, what the hell, they'll do. 'On my desk' my fat hairy ass. Haven't had a desk since I was in college."

He was working, he said, on two things. "One's a piece of sausage. Some rich hardware dude out in the Valley who always wanted to make movies, figures vampires had their day, then zombies, next big thing has to be mermaids and—men. You'd be surprised how well Joseph Conrad adapts. I'm throwing in Little Nell for good measure. Other one's a fine piece of cod for some pale Norwegian type who wants to show us what America's all about."

Another incoming call sounded on Manny's line. He was gone seven seconds, tops. "Told 'em to fuck off. So you're telling me you just walked away?"

"You got it. House. Car. That life."

"What now?"

"Who knows. I'm in the wind. See where it takes me, I guess."

"Has a certain ring to it, doesn't it? Been here before. Nietzsche's eternal return and all that shit." The call alert sounded again. This time, Manny ignored it. "You could come on back out here. Fresh out of fatted calves, but I'd gladly buy you a plate of pork and yucca."

"And I'll do that. Soon. But for now—"

"Yeah, sure. Just be careful. Things may not be as easy as they used to be. Some of it comes back, some doesn't."

Driver looked around. His couples were gone. A younger crowd seemed to be moving in now, wagging their iPods and cellphones behind them, fatally connected.

Why had he called Manny in the first place? We talk up our problems to others, odds are high we're doing it either to reassure ourselves that what we're doing is right or to talk ourselves into doing something we know is stupid.

Yeah, he thought—that about covers it.

Wondering about motivations, why he or anybody else did what they did, was something he did his best to steer clear of. How the hell could you ever know? Act, when it was called for. Otherwise, hang back.

And the next act here, for him, had to be wheels.

There was, of course, a huge parking lot filled with cars just outside, any one of which could be his. And he wouldn't hesitate, if it became necessary.

But for now it wasn't.

I should have figured this out a long time ago, Bill thought. Life could have been a hell of a lot simpler. Now he could say and do as he pleased. The manners he'd been raised with; that sensitivity stuff he'd later had to learn, having to put up with other people's shit whether he wanted to or not—all of it was out the door, down the block and gone.

Now he could just stare at Wendell when he asked if Bill would be wanting to go out and sit with the others, watch some TV, play cards, they'd like that. Didn't have to react at all if he didn't want to. They'd put it down like everything else to *Mr. Bill's not quite with us today.* The Alzheimer's or whatever it was they thought he had.

In a way they were right. The world out there, the one they lived in, was just pills and bad food and waiting. It smelled bad. But the world he carried around with him, that one was rich with people he'd known, places he'd been, things he'd done. The pictures there still moved.

Thing is, he liked Wendell. And he wondered if maybe Wendell knew what was going on with him.

Sometimes when Bill sat there not responding, Wendell would look him in the eye and grin. Like a month back, something like that, when the "weekly entertainment" was a folk singer. Bill hated the fucking sixties, and here it was, standing in front of him. Long hair, tie-dye shirt, a smile that made you want to knock him silly. Sillier than he already was. Laughing at his own jokes. Pretending to flirt with the old women in the front row.

The guy's first song started 'My life is a river,' Bill thinking the hell it is, my life's like my head, nothing but dry fallen leaves in there. It's not over, Eli said again and again, his oldest friend and the only one besides Billie who visited him. But it was, or well nigh.

He'd looked over and seen Wendell watching him.

Still, last night had been, by their standards, huge. Roommate Bobby's daughter had smuggled in Bobby's favorite, Girl Scout cookies and a pint of Early Times bourbon. It wasn't in the rule book, but they weren't supposed to have alcohol here. The list of reasons went on and on: confusion, dehydration, medication interactions, livers already sorely abused. Bill and Bobby finished the cookies in short order, drew out the bourbon, one sip at a time.

Now Bill sat watching the garbage truck start-and-stop down the street outside. Liquid poured out its backside. Looked like a giant snail, extruding a track of slime behind as it moved slowly along.

Three hours till lunch.

The car came off a lot hanging on to the edge of Tempe by its toenails. He'd been buzzed by two salesmen, one twentyish and enthusiastic, all but bouncing on his toes, the other with something of the crocodile about him, ageless, enduring, who dropped away as he moved ever deeper into the used section. What you want is a ride that doesn't show its colors, one that never growls, just snaps. As he came back the second time to a Ford Fairlane, a young tire kicker in fatigues and baseball cap hollered over at him: "Hey, zero to sixty, with that one you might wanna take a book along, read while you wait, you know what I'm saying?"

He popped the hood again. Moments later a pair of well worn khaki trousers came into view. The crocodile. He waited till Driver straightened, then smiled. "I'm afraid someone's been under the hood there, kinda messed it up some."

Driver had the hood back down and was counting out money before he finished his sentence.

Someone had been under there all right, someone who knew what he was doing. And what that someone had started, Driver finished up in a garage at the butt end of Van Buren.

Half a century ago the main drag for Phoenix and a watering hole for those travelling U.S. Highways 70, 80 and 89, Van Buren was now a dusty long drawl of swayback motels, streetwalkers, abandoned storefronts and vacant lots overgrown with rubbish, the very image of everything used up, worn out, cast off. The city had moved on and left this dry husk behind.

Boyd's Garage hadn't fared a lot better, but it had held on—since 1948, according to the sign whose ancient letters and numbers had been recently over-painted. This was done free-handed, so that crescents and dimples of aqua ghosted the tomato-red edges. In harsh sunlight the new brush strokes showed wide and crude.

Inside, afloat on the reek of grease, cleanser, exhaust fumes, gasoline, hair oil and male cologne, all was untouched by the years passing outside. The wall by the office (long unused, to judge by the stacks of boxes inside) was shingled with girlie calendars, some of them dating back to WWII. The top of the antique Coke machine opened onto horizontal steel slats. You put your money in and slid a bottle along slats to the gate, fished it out by the neck. The bottom was filled with cool water of uncertain vintage. Didn't pay to look too closely, no telling what might be swimming down in there.

The Fairlane was a street car, no doubt about it. And the owner had taken pains to make it look unprepossessing, which made Driver wonder if the owner could have been someone like him, someone doing, in some shape or form, what he used to do. Just as he wondered how the car came to wind up on that lot among the sheep. And why no one had recognized it for what it was.

Or had they?

Once Driver had paid for the car, he asked to see a mechanic.

"You do understand—"

"I just want to talk to him. And not a service manager. One of the guys with grease lines in his hands he can't get rid of."

He'd driven the car around back and gone in. Luis glanced at the car over his shoulder, then gave Driver a look before nodding.

So he knew.

Driver asked, and Luis told him about Boyd's. Man named Matthew Sweet owned it, Sweet Matt everyone called him, him and his wife Lupa, they'd rent out time, a bay, tools, whatever he needed. Good people there, he said. To go with your good car.

It all took Driver back: the smells, poking about in the Fairlane's innards, sliding under and out and under again, tearing a gash in his hand when a wrench slipped, Spanish tumbling off the walls around him.

Back to his early days, when he was first finding his skills in garages much like this one, and at the makeshift track in the desert between Tucson and Phoenix. Herb was the beginning of it, an outsider like him who he befriended at school and for whom engines, transmissions, and suspensions were living, breathing things. Then Jorge and his family and the family's friends, which amounted to most of the population of South Tucson. That had been the first time Driver ever felt like he fit in anywhere.

He remembered Manny back when he was on one of his favorite harangues about words and misuse of same. They were drinking in a dive out by LAX, a self-styled blues bar, some guy playing guitar with his teeth at two in the afternoon for an audience of four dedicated drunks, a hooker, a couple of Japanese businessmen in suits, and them. Manny'd slammed back another glass of wine and taken a sudden turn.

"You ever look at a thesaurus? One-third of the damn thing is index. That's the way our lives are. We spend a third of it trying to figure out the other two-thirds." You never knew what was going on in there with Manny.

With anyone, really.

Like that guy over by the Coke machine, shaved eyebrows and head, jailyard stance, forested with tattoos. Looked like a thousand he'd known. Only this guy's tattoos were all religious—he was walking stained glass—and he had the sweet smile of a child.

"It's like everything else in life," Manny had said yesterday on the phone. "You have to decide what you want, else you just keep spinning around, circling the drain. You want to get away from the guys?"

"Sure I do."

"Or you want to put them down?" He waited, then laughed. "Well, there it is, then. We ponder and weigh and debate. While in silence, somewhere back in the darkness behind words, our decisions are made."

Driver wasn't sure he'd ever made a decision, not in the sense Manny meant. You stayed loose and when the time came, you looked around, saw what was there, went with it. Not that you let things push you, but you moved faster with the current than against. It was like reading signs, following spoor.

Manny of course would insist that such claims were BS that bore the stain of religion.

"Signs? What bleedin' signs? What, someone put up speed limits, cattle crossings?" Anything not completely rational, for Manny it was the religious impulse incognito or in drag. That day at the blues bar he'd got onto atheists.

"Worse than Christians. So dead certain and full of themselves. Got their own little religion going, don't they. Own set of rituals, psalms, Hanukkahs, hosannahs. Can't say a word to them they'll hear."

Then, in his usual hopscotch, dropping in random accents and cadences from scripts he'd recently worked on:

"Free will, my hairy ass. What we believe, books we hold in high regard, hell, even the music we listen to—it's all programmed, my boy, burned into us by heredity, background, what we're exposed to till it takes. We think we make choices. But what happens is the choices walk up, stand face to face with us, and stare us down."

"So you believe a man's path, the way of his life, is set?"

"Re: belief, see above. But yes, we come suddenly alive, we scamper around like a cockroach when lights go on, and then the light goes off."

"That's damned bleak, Manny."

"No argument here. But those moments of light, as we scamper—they can be glorious."

A decision? Maybe when he'd come above ground. But, really, hadn't he drifted there too? Fetched up in an apartment out in Mesa with enough of a cut from the last job that he needn't worry about getting back to work any time soon. Everything close to the ground and earth-colored, sky stretched out for miles overhead and all around, bright baking sun, shadows with edges like blades. Walking to meals, he passed an upholstery shop, two churches, Happy Trails Motel, a quick-serve oil and lube, BJ's Hobby & Stamp Store, a Thai restaurant the size of a house trailer, apartment complex after apartment complex with names like Desert Palms, filling stations, used tire shops, Rainbow Donuts. What first had seemed to him exotic—from another world, quite literally—began to take on the tincture and unremarked weight of the familiar.

For a time it felt almost as though he were back in foster homes, as though he'd been dropped into yet another temporary location. Any moment they'd come retrieve him, take him elsewhere.

A week went by. Then another. Waitresses knew him by sight now. Cooks having a smoke out back of the Thai place waved as he passed.

Somewhere in there, halfway down a block perhaps, or while crossing a street, somewhere between one first light and nightfall, he realized this was it, he wasn't going back to the old life.

He was 26, and on his way to becoming Paul West.

Twenty-six, with no employment history to speak of, no references, no commercial skills and few enough social ones. One thing he knew. He knew cars.

In the town of Guadalupe, a small Hispanic and Native American community between Tempe and Phoenix, he found a garage with a spare bay to rent. Mostly, they did customizing—paint jobs, rockers, lifts, your basic muscle-car calls—and he started off catching overflow and stuff the others didn't want to do. A heads-up to Felix brought in a private job or two, then more. The other mechanics noticed, watched and spread the word, and before he knew it he had more work than he could handle. Gradually he was able to back off the add-on work and concentrate on restorations. He put a couple of classics together, a Hudson and a British roadster, then built a commissioned racer to specs from the ground up. The check from that one got him thinking about other possibilities.

He scouted out a garage with a large storage space that could be turned into an office, in the ramshackle industrial section just south of downtown. Once part of a chain, the place had been abandoned for years, and he got it for next to nothing. Started off buying, refurbishing and selling classic cars. Then, having built up a decent inventory—he wasn't part of it anymore, and didn't want to be, but he knew how things worked out there—he built up a rental service to Hollywood studios. They needed a Terraplane or vintage Rolls, Paul West had one, in fine shape and camera-ready.

Paul West also had a secretary and two employees. And Driver wondered sometimes how they were holding out, what they were doing. Maybe they'd figure a way to take over the business, keep it up and running.

Five days pretty much nonstop and he had the Fairlane where he wanted it.

Kind of place it was, the others stayed cool, left him to his work, but they'd been watching.

"Righteous," a voice said from somewhere above size-10 BKs that came up over the ankles and had so many colors to them they looked like clown puke.

Driver rolled out from under. Short guy, white—whiter than Driver—but he spoke the local Spanish like a native and knew everyone. Family, maybe. Not a regular, but he'd been around.

"You figuring on flying that shit to Mars or what?"

"It needed a little work."

"A little work's not what you did, friend. What you did was take Gramma's sweet ride and turn it into something's gonna be out there looking for meat six times a day. You could hang a building off that trans, the torque it'll take now."

"Maybe I got a little carried away."

"And carried the wheel base up a notch or two with you, from the look of it. Cut-and-fill?"

"More like hack-and-fill, but yeah, it'll stay on the ground. Somebody'd already started the job, I finished it."

"Nose?"

Driver nodded. "Wheels moved forward. Ditched the front suspension for a straight axle, buggy springs."

"Four-barrel?"

"Right. It's Seventies. Four-barrel standard, 429 cubes."

"Smooth. And sweet as cream." He reached out and patted the car tenderly on the rear fender, the way one would a horse's flank. The third finger was missing. Rings on all the others. "Looks like the desert and a long moonlight ride's gonna be whispering in your ear 'bout any day now."

"Definitely on the list of things that could happen."

"When it does, you have yourself a good ride, every minute of it."

"I'll do that."

"Best times of your life, just you and the road, leaving all the rest of this shit behind."

"I hear you."

The man nodded a half inch or so and walked away.

Were they the best times? In many ways, absolutely. Out there loose and free and moving fast, away from everything that works so hard to hold you in place. Once you had that feeling, once it soaked into your bones, you never got over it, and nothing else ever came close.

But sooner or later, as Manny always reminded him, you had to pull over and get out of the car.

He'd barely got back under when a second set of shoes, pink hightops well-smeared with grease this time, hove into view and didn't go away. He rolled out. She worked at the far end, by the vertical door that stayed propped open on fifty-gallon drums. Everyone called her Billie or just B. Strictly business, from what he'd seen. Hispanic, but second, third generation.

"Yes ma'am?"

First she looked startled. Then she laughed.

"Sweet ride, but how'll it fit in, there in Scottsdale?"

"Any luck at all, she'll never have to find out."

"*She*, huh?"

He waited what actors would call two beats and said, "Yes, ma'am."

She laughed again and waved toward the hood. When he told her to be his guest, she popped it. Came up for air shaking her head.

"That's some serious head room."

"Never know what you might need."

"Right, and when you think you do, it usually turns out to be the wrong thing." Her fingers had left a smudge on the hood. Noticing, she bent to wipe it with her shirt tail. A man's denim shirt, well faded, sleeves rolled to her biceps. Loose khaki-colored cargo pants. "I wouldn't mind taking that for a ride."

His turn to laugh.

"Guess you heard that one before," she said.

"Once or twice. Not in this context."

She looked around. "Some context we got here. This the part where the music comes up, you know, strings and shit?"

"Probably not."

"Yeah, probably not."

◇◇◇

In addition to oleanders, crickets and cracks, the new place had a TV, and as he sat there that night finishing up his carry-out Bento Box from Tokyo Express with hot air blowing from window to window and the swamp cooler heaving, local news gave way to a movie and suddenly he was looking into Shannon's face.

Part of his face, actually—seen in a rearview mirror. But it was him. Shannon was the best stunt driver who ever lived, a legend really, and the one who'd given Driver a leg up, got him into the business. Bought him meals, even let him sleep on his couch. Ten months after Driver's first solid job, on a routine stunt like hundreds he'd done before, Shannon's car went off a cliff, somersaulted twice, and sat rocking on its back like a beetle, cameras rolling the whole time.

This movie was titled *Stranger*, about the self-appointed guardian of a small community. You never saw him, just his car, a Mercury, pulling up at an overlook or turning in behind a suspicious vehicle, and once in a while his arm in the window, a shadowy profile or a slice of face in the mirror, or his back and neck as he sat watching. You never found out what the man's motivations were. The movie had been made on the cheap, so instead of an actor they'd just used Shannon for those bits. There was kick ass driving all through. Not much of a script, when you got right down to it. But the movie had that sheen that cheap films often have when the makers are shooting something they believe in, working with next to no money, time, or resources, reaching hard for effect.

Had to be an old movie, since Shannon, the parts of Shannon he could see anyway, looked young. Probably made by youngsters with little more than a gleam in their eyes and a credit card. They'd be huge now or selling real estate somewhere.

That night, as a predicted rain eased down outside, memories mixed with twisted versions of scenes from the movie in his dreams. The next day he caught the Crown Vic in the rear view and realized what it meant, he almost laughed.

No doubt about its following him. Late model, nondescript gray, two men. He'd turned off Indian School, swung up to Osborn, then onto Sixteenth and they were still there. He took a residential street, one that looked wide and inviting but that, at the end of a long, curving block, ran headlong into a maze of apartment complexes and curlicue feeders. He'd come across it months ago and from sheer force of habit filed the location away. The area was riddled with stubs of pavement abutting the street, where private driveways had been before the complexes took over. Accelerating and taking a turn or two, just enough to get out ahead, he backed into one of those stubs and shut off the engine. Cars were parked along the streets on both sides—another plus. Across from him two young men unloaded furniture looking to be mostly veneer from a van that dipped alarmingly each time one of them climbed aboard.

DOS AMIGOS MOVERS
WE GET THE JOB DONE

Driver got out and walked over.

"Give you a hand there?"

They looked at him, then at one another, and right-fully so, with suspicion. One was crowding six foot, light complected with startlingly black hair that swept to either side like a crow's wings. The other was short and deeply brown, hair sparse but long, upper arms like bags filled with rocks.

"I live just up the block." Driver hooked his head. "Back there. Work at home, fourteen-fifteen hours a day I'm nose to nose with a computer screen. Then I got to get out, move around some. You know?"

"We can't pay you, friend." This from the shorter one, who seemed more or less to be in charge and more or less to be doing the lion's share of the heavy lifting.

"Don't expect it."

Moments later, as Driver came down the ramp with an end table in one hand, lamp in the other, he saw the Crown Vic cruise past at a slow trot. It pulled up by the Fairlane, the passenger got out and checked, looked around, got back in. Never did more than glance across at three poor slobs unloading furniture. The Crown Vic came back by twice as they emptied the van, four minutes or so between laps, so they were sweeping the complexes, looking hard for whatever signs they thought they might see. Last lap, the guy on the passenger side was talking on a phone. The Crown Vic picked up speed and was gone.

"Better get back to it, I guess," Driver said.

"Back in the saddle, right. Hey, man—much thanks for the help. Cold beer in the cooler up front if you want one."

"Next time."

"*Any* time."

Two days later he's sitting at the mall swallowing bitter coffee when the guy at the next table says "You've made Carl unhappy."

Driver looked over. Thirtyish, dress shirt and slacks, could be a sales rep on break or the manager of Dillard's across the way.

"Carl is good at one thing and one thing only. That is pretty much his life. But you lost him."

"I take it Carl drives a grey Crown Vic."

"And when Carl's unhappy, it's like...well, it's as though small black clouds spring up everywhere." He held up his cup. "Grabbing a refill, get you anything?"

"I'm good."

While the man was gone, a couple of teenagers took the table. He came back and stood there silently until they got up and moved away. He sat down. Some kind of slush drink, so that he kept tilting his head back, letting the soft ice slide down his throat.

"You and Carl of the Black Cloud, I assume you'd both have the same business address."

"More or less."

Pretty much, more or less: evidently his visitor came from a world of approximations, one where perception, judgment, even facts, were in suspension, and could shift at a moment's notice.

A security guard strolled by, walkie-talkie in hand, pant legs six inches too long in the crotch and well chewed at the bottom. Driver heard "down by the food court, be about," then he was gone.

"And what business might that be?"

"Diversified, actually." Again the man's head went back as the cup tilted. A thin line of red slush ran down his jaw.

"For the moment it seems to be me."

"For the moment."

"I don't much care for being followed," Driver said.

"Few of us would." He looked off at two teenagers walking out of Spencer's. One would push the other, who'd stagger off, come back and push him. They kept at this as they proceeded down the mall. Both wore hightops without laces. "You think about stuff much? Why you're here, what it all means?"

"Not really."

"Yeah. Knew a guy back in law school, more years ago than I want to think about, that did. Boy thought he was going to change the world. All he had to do first, was get to what the problems were, you know?"

"He ever figure it out?"

"We'd have to dig him up and ask. Second year, he went off the fourth-floor balcony."

Driver heard ice rasping at the cup as the man swirled it and peered inside.

"Some people look at what happens to them and they think, there's something *responsible*, some invisible agent behind all this, moving things around, causing things to happen."

"Coherence," Driver said.

"What?"

"Coherence. What they're looking for."

"I guess. Then others look at the same thing and see the purposelessness of it all. That there are only lame explanations, or none. No reason or reasons behind it. Things just happen. Life, death. Everything."

Driver finished his coffee, stood looking around for the nearest trash receptacle. It was by the column where his visitor sat. He started that way.

"As I said, I don't much care for being followed. I particularly don't like having people close to me killed."

The man smiled and said, "Lie down with dogs..." That was the last thing he said. As he tilted his head back, Driver swung around from the trash receptacle, fingers tucked, middle knuckle extended, and struck him in the throat. He felt the trachea give way and fold in on itself, watched surprise hit the man's face, then his first gasps for air.

As the man slumped and looked about wildly, as he grasped for the table and slid down it, hands at last letting go just before he hit the floor, Driver walked away.

On impulse he swung out onto I-10 and tooled down past Tempe, through Ahwatukee and Casa Grande, to Tucson. Hour and twenty minutes with the new 75-mph speed limit, then you hit town and spent damn near as long inching down Speedway or Grant. Lots of empty buildings where small shops used to be, specialty clothing, hobbies and games, pool service centers, tax preparers. A row of five or six room-sized abandoned restaurants, home-cooking, Thai, Mexican, Lebanese, daily specials still painted on windows.

He pulled up in front of the old house. If they still lived here, they'd spent some of the money on fixing up the place. A new driveway, one without the edges that had crumbled away like old cornbread and the long cracks spilling over with green shoots and ant colonies. New wooden gate to the backyard and, back there, what looked to be a room added on. Dark red-dish tiles on the roof.

Chances were good they'd moved on, of course. Maybe they weren't even alive anymore. But then again, maybe they *were* still here. Tucson didn't have

the shifting-sands population of its neighbor to the
northwest; here, people took root.

He thought of Mrs. Smith's thinning hair, how she'd
spend half an hour each morning brushing it out and
spraying it with dollar-store hairspray to make it look
fuller. He remembered the tiny stifling attic room that
was his. How seldom Mr. Smith spoke and, when he
did, how apologetically, as though embarrassed to
be asking from the world what he knew to be fully
unearned attention.

So here he sat, not in a classic Stingray this time but in
an old Ford. He looked around at the stands of saguaro,
rock-garden front lawns, the Catalina Mountains in the
distance, and remembered thinking how there were these
places in the world where nothing much ever changes,
civilization's tide pools. And after eight or nine years he
still remembered every word of the note he'd left when
he dropped off Nino's money and Doc's cat.

> *Her name is Miss Dickinson. I can't say she
> belonged to a friend of mine who just died, since
> cats don't belong to anyone, but the two of them
> walked the same hard path, side by side, for a
> long time. She deserves to spend the last years
> of her life in some security. So do you. Please
> take care of Miss Dickinson, just as you did
> me, and please accept this money in the spirit
> it's offered. I always felt bad about taking your*

*car when I left. Never doubt that I appreciate
what you did for me.*

He sat with the engine idling at a purr, wondering how many neighbors stood behind curtains and blinds peering out. A hummingbird fell from nowhere and hovered by his open window, framed perfectly, before again rocketing away. Nor was *he* one to remain long in place or past. Always another open road ahead. And much to get done back in Phoenix.

Going downstream, Phoenix to Tucson, there was the blackened, corkscrew-gnarled, unimaginably old saguaro that got decorated with broad red ribbons each Christmas, and that made him smile every time he saw it. Heading back, he always watched out for signs alongside the orchards just short of the half-way mark. Picacho Peak had seen the westernmost battle of the Civil War, when Union cavalry came upon a group of Confederates on their way to warn the Tucson garrison of Union encroachment. Yearly reenactments of the battle included cavalry, infantry, and artillery units—a far cry from the twenty-three horsemen and ninety-minute duration of the original. The area also hosted one of three units of the state prison at Florence.

So, back up the road, toward Picacho, past signs discreetly warning that hitchhikers might be escaped prisoners.

Driver thinking, Aren't we all?

Road signs bore the marks of old target practice. Birds burrowed into the cactus and built nests there.

Bill's eyes came open. He'd spent a lot of time lying awake trying to decide whether that ceiling was green or gray. And wondering why they would build ceilings so high in a place where people were steadily shrinking.

From down the hall came the smell of weak coffee, and behind that the smell of what had been spilled on the warmer plate and was now burning. Two staff members stood just outside his room talking about what they did last night. The food cart delivering breakfast to those unable to make it to the dining room limped and banged along on its bad wheel. Shortly after settling in, Bill had offered to fix the wheel. They looked at him oddly and said thank you but they had someone to do things like that. He soon got used to that look. And apparently their someone was hard to find.

Gray. Green. Who the fuck cared. One of his early partners, who'd been a William too, so he was Bill and the partner got to be Billy, everyone called them Bill Squared—Billy had painted his house all beige. Everything. Outside, inside, every wall. Beige couch. Beige curtains. Over the years he'd swear Billy had become beige himself.

That was what being in this place was like.

In the dream from which he awakened, the bullets had struck softly, dimpling, then casting up puffs of dust and debris. They made soft pops, like the sound of lips being pulled gently apart.

The bullets (my bullets, as he always thought of them, the ones intended for me) had gone into the wall to his left and right. The shooter was nervous and new at this. The shooter was twelve years old.

That wasn't how it happened, soft, slow. In life it happened fast. In an instant. But in the dream it got stretched, extended, elongated, it just went on and on...like his life here.

Dream. Memory. Who the fuck cared.

Once it was over, his partner was bleeding out and the kid lay dead by the wall.

Back when Driver was first discovering his gift, first realizing that cars and his life were inextricably intertwined, whenever things went wrong, with the family, one of the kids, or within the community, Jorge's abuela would say, "You've seen the tip of the wolf's ear." Over the years he'd seen his share of ear tips, and of wolves.

He was at Boyd's, fine-tuning the Ford following the Tucson jaunt. Outside, day gave way to night by a kind of gentlemen's agreement, neither losing face: light still strong as shadows moved in from nearby hills and taller buildings. Pushing out from under the car he saw that, while the radio blared and lights blazed and tools lay where they had been in use, on floors and benches and hoods, he was alone. The other mechanics and workers and hangers-on were gone.

Instinctively he got to his feet, taking a long socket wrench with him.

What was it about these guys going around in pairs?

One stayed by the door as the other stepped toward him. Rail-thin, musculature standing out on his arms like add-ons. Never glanced at the wrench, but halfway across he held up his hands palm out.

Driver moved out from the car. Don't want your back to the wall.

"A word, young man, nothing more. We're not a threat." Keeping the one hand in place, palm out, he stepped sideways to lower the radio's volume. Accordion, fiddle, and guitarron fell away from the ear, became almost internal, part of the heartbeat.

"You had a pleasant trip earlier today?"

Driver nodded. Getting weirder all the time.

"While you were gone, you had callers. Left to their own wiles, and for no good reason—nothing to look for, nothing to find—they made a mess of your most recent home. A mistake those two will not be making again."

His eyes went momentarily around the garage, taking it all in, then to the Fairlane.

"The car does not look like much."

"That's not what she's about."

The man dipped his head in affirmation. The skin on his forehead was deeply pleated, ridges that ran from his eyes right up to his hairline. You could plant crops in there.

"These men, the ones who came into your home, were expendable. Coins to be tossed. The ones who sent them, those with substance, are displeased with you."

"I suspect they're displeased with a lot of things."

"There is that. But, first the man at the mall. Now these two."

"With which I had nothing to do."

"Those who sent them will assume otherwise."

Driver was shifting around, watching both men closely, their reactions, body language, eyes. "What am I to these people?"

"A danger, imagined or otherwise? An irritant? An imperfection? Something to be removed. But—" His eyes followed Driver's to the one posted at the door—"I don't speak for them."

Looking back, he moved slowly toward the Fairlane as Driver circled away, and rested a hand momentarily on the car's hood.

"They have a smell to them, don't they," he said, "the good ones."

Carefully he lifted the windshield wiper, tucked a card beneath, and eased it down.

"Mr. Beil asks that you have dinner with him. The time and address are on the card. He asks that I tell you it will be the best meal of your life."

"I don't—"

"Be hungry, Mr. West."

Driver watched them leave, heard the car spit and catch and pull away. Momentarily the others began drifting in by various passways, all eyes going first to Driver. Soon the music was back up, the clangs and revs and burr of power tools back in place.

The card was thick stock, light blue with embossed silver letters, just the name, James Beil. Inscribed on the back in handwriting every bit as precise as the printing:

Fifth Corner, off 16th Ave, 9 p.m. A little over two hours away.

"Everything good?" It was the guy with the clown-puke BKs.

"*Está bien.*"

"We were not far. We were watching, all of us."

Like most statements, Driver thought, you could read it more than one way. But he nodded and said that was good to hear.

The man started off but, before Driver could put down the wrench, turned. "We had your back, is what I mean to say."

Beil lifted his cup. Steam passed like a sweep of rain across his glasses. He blinked. "Do you know who I am?"

"Not the sous chef, I take it."

"Hardly."

"No clue, then."

"Good. As it should be." He downed a slug of the coffee. "Something we appear to have in common." He drank again and set the cup down empty. "Among other things, I own this restaurant. I've taken the liberty of ordering for you, thought we might have a drink first. Your preference is single malt, I believe." A waiter stepped up carrying a crystal tumbler. "From Orkney. This Scotch has spent an appreciable time in its cask. Waiting, as it were?"

Driver lifted the glass in thanks and sipped, held it in his mouth.

"Age twelve, you watched your mother kill your father. You then lived for four years with a couple named Smith in Tucson—they are still in the house, by the way. Leaving with no good-byes, you became a stunt driver in L.A., one of the best, they say. I have seen your work, and would agree. It was the *other* career that didn't go so well.

"You fall away from sight at that point, leaving bodies behind this time instead of a home. You surface a bit later, a new day, a new city, as Paul West. Years pass and again you vanish, only to pop up—or to stay low, it might better be said—here.

"Ah…and here it is."

Driver thinking back to what Felix said, *they know more about me than anyone should*, as waiters lowered plates and platters onto the table. A pasta dish with clams, veal in a wine sauce studded with bright red peppers and capers, a cutting board of prosciutto and cheeses, a bowl of salad. Glasses set out for white and red wines. Sparkling water.

"Eat. Please."

Driver tried to remember the last time he had done so. He'd had a breakfast burrito, what, yesterday, eleven or so in the morning? Once he'd served himself, the waiters conveyed the platters down the table to Beil, who spooned out small portions from each. They ate without speaking. Sounds gradually subsided past the doors to this private dining room.

"The restaurant is closing early tonight," Beil said.

Looking around, Driver realized that the waiters had withdrawn. They were alone.

Beil finished with a final bite of salad, placed the fork on his plate diagonally, and crossed it with his knife. He poured himself fresh tea from a tulip-shaped pitcher. Sweet tea in the Southern fashion, Driver had discovered. He'd put the glass down and not touched it since.

"I grew up in Texas," Beil said. "Not in the piney woods and not in any town, but in the wild, unclaimed stretches—unclaimable, really. Bare land every way you looked, and the horizon so far off it may as well have been The Great Hereafter. My mother and father were there but forever busy, he as foreman for one of the huge ranches, she as librarian for the county library in the nearest town. I had my room at the rear of the house, all but a separate domicile, and there I went about feeling my way along the years, putting together a life from pieces of things, shiny things, discarded things, useless things, that I found around me, much as a bird builds its nest.

"In many ways it was like living in another country, another world. Even the air was different. The wind would shift, and you'd smell cattle, their rankness, their manure, coming from the ranch where my father worked, miles and miles away. Smells of earth, mold, stale water, and rot as well. And dust. Always the smell of dust. I'd lie in bed at night in absolute darkness thinking this might be a little what it was like being buried. I knew I had to get out of there."

A crash sounded far off, back in the kitchen perhaps. Beil's eyes didn't go to the sound, but a smile came close to touching down on his lips. "Do you believe that some are born with a proclivity, a talent? For music, say, or for leadership?"

Driver nodded. "Only a few find it."

"Exactly. Mine, I realized early on, was for problem solving. But I was also something of a contrarian, not as much interested in confronting problems as I was in finding a way *around* them. It would have made of me an extremely poor scientist, the discipline at which I first dabbled, but in other pursuits....Well, there you are, as they say."

"And here I am."

"Wondering why, no doubt."

"It was an interesting invitation."

"We work with what we have. You once drove, and now you drive again. Is that recidivism? Adaptive behavior? Or simply returning to what you are?"

"*Yes* would probably answer all those."

"People attempting to kill you might well be construed a problem."

"For which you have the solution."

"Not at all. The problem is yours." All sound from the restaurant had ceased. Through a small pane of glass in the door Driver saw the lights go out. "A solution, though—this could be another thing we have in common."

Afterward, he drove to South Mountain. Well past eleven, and not a lot of activity out here, two or three convenience stores, a scatter of Mexican drive-throughs along Baseline. He found a boulder halfway up and sat looking down at the city's lights. Planes came and went from the airport ten or twelve miles away, ripples in the dark and silence and boundless sky.

Driver didn't want to go back to the new place, trashed or not. He couldn't think of any place he did want to go. What he wanted was to get back in the car and drive. Drive away from all this. Or just drive. Like the guy back at the garage had said: just you and the road, leaving all the rest of this shit behind.

But he couldn't. And what Beil had proposed— once they'd snaked past *I work alone* and *They'll keep coming*—seemed, if not the best alternative, then certainly a feasible one.

"The people who engaged me—"

"As a problem solver."

"Exactly. Like all of us, primarily they wish to restore order, to have things the way they were. But now there are imbalances. Problems with those moving the pieces around."

"None of which has anything to do with me."

"Your presence has introduced wholly unexpected variables. You've become a crux, of a sort."

Driver's attention went to what looked to be a collision down on Baseline. First, headlights moving toward one another too fast, then a hitch in time, then the lights gone suddenly askew. Did he hear the crash, a horn, seconds later? He remembered a night years ago back in L.A. when he sat in Manny's banged-to-hell Mercedes on the northern flank of Baldwin Hills, in oil fields that appeared deserted but might for all he knew still be functioning. The gate was open, and they'd entered along a dirt road. The entire city lay before them. Santa Monica, the Wilshire District, downtown. Hollywood Hills in the distance.

"The diminutive fires of the planet," Manny had said. "What Neruda called them. All those lights. The ones inside you, too. Your house is burning, that's all you see. But get up here, get some distance, it's just another tiny fire.

"We go through our lives agonizing over income or what others think, getting wound up about Betty LaButt's new CD, who shot or fucked Insert-name-here on some TV show, or the latest skinny on the latest idiot with cheekbones who's making a run for office, and all the while, governments go on killing their citizens, children die from food additives and advertising, women get beaten or worse, meth labs now take over the rural south the way kudzu once did, and we're getting lies spoon fed to us at every turn.

"The most interesting thing about us as a species may be all the ways we figure out so we don't have to think about those things."

This from a the man who spent most of his life writing crap movies. Well, mostly crap anyway.

Emergency vehicles pulled in below, so yes, a collision.

Driver stood. The boulder he'd been sitting on was all but covered with paint-sprayed tags, scribblings, and knife etchings—Manny would have insisted upon calling them modern petroglyphs. In the dark Driver could only make out that they were there, not distinguish them. Tags, he figured, tags and hearts and dates and jumbled-up names. And if he could read them, they'd make about as much sense as everything else.

He drove back in along Southern and Buckeye, then spilled over to Van Buren and, surprised to see lights on at the garage, turned in. The door was unlocked. As he stepped through, a head leaned out from behind the hood of a bottle-green BMW.

"Everything all right?" he said.

"Would I be under here if it was?"

"I mean…" He looked around. The only lights were two floods over her space. Strange to have the place so silent. "It's late."

"And quiet."

His face must have carried the question.

"You tilted your head, the way people do when they're listening—just for a second there. Nice, isn't it?"

He nodded.

"Love it. Being alone in the night, nothing much else in the world except what I'm working on." She came out from behind the BMW. "I have a key. Lupa's daughter and I, we went to school together. Anyway, this monster's almost done."

"Yours?"

"No way I could afford it. Or want it. But I can get it running smooth again, and the guy who owns it can't do that. You notice the sidewalks just up the way?"

"Not really."

"WPA, from 1928. More cracks than cement, so the city finally decides to repair them. One look and you can tell the old good stuff from the new crappy stuff."

"I've got some poorly repaired cracks myself."

"Not the right vintage."

"A *little* earlier, true. Interesting thing to notice about the neighborhood."

"Everything's interesting. You just have to look closely."

"And most people don't."

She shrugged. "Their loss."

He was careful not to move closer. And while she seemed wholly at ease, body language told him she was every bit as watchful and aware. "I'm sorry, I don't remember your name."

"You never had it."

Caught without a response, he shook his head.

"You have legal motives in mind, say—oh, I don't know, applying for a marriage license, checking my credit—put down Stephanie. Real life, I'm Billie. Long story, not very interesting."

"I thought everything was."

She turned to put down the feeler gauge she was holding and turned back. "You have possibilities, Eight."

When he held his hands out and apart in mock supplication, she pointed to the stall where he usually worked. Right. Number eight.

They turned to the door in unison.

"You folks okay?" Floating in the gray behind concentric circles of blinding light, the cop stepped in. He pivoted the flashlight around the garage, up and down, then back to them before shutting it off. As their eyes readjusted, his partner came into sight at the door.

"Saw the lights on, commercial establishment. Kinda late, isn't it?"

"And quiet," Driver said.

The lead cop let that go. His eyes did a once-over, checking Driver's hands, clothing, shoes, stance.

"We're good, Officer," Billie said. "I often work late."

"Yes, ma'am, we've seen your lights on before. What about your friend here?"

"He works here too."

"Sure he does." The cop flipped his light back on, ran it along the BMW, shut it off. "You have papers on that car?"

"It's a repair job, Officer, almost done. That's what we do here. I can give you the name and number of the owner if you'd like."

"Might need that. Right now, I'm gonna need to see some ID."

Driver's hesitation before reaching for his wallet was instinctive and fleeting. He didn't think it showed. But afterwards he wondered if somehow Billie hadn't caught it. She stepped toward the cop, pulling a drivers license out of the rear pocket of her jeans. The license was as well-worn as the jeans.

The cop took it, looked up at her, then back to the license.

"You Bill Cooper's kid? The one in, what, law school?"

"At ASU, yes sir." She held out her hand. He gave her the license. It went back in the rear pocket.

He stood a moment, glanced at Driver one more time, and said, "Sorry to disturb you, ma'am." The two of them walked out. Driver heard both doors, heard the car start up. The cops had parked some distance from the garage.

"Wasn't *that* interesting," Billie said. "Broke the monotony of just another night running up someone's bill, sopping up more grease, hanging out with a dude that came in off the street."

She stepped almost up to him. The awareness was still there, but the watchfulness, for whatever reason, was gone.

"Could you do with a cup of coffee, piece of pie, something on that order? There's a place up the street. If it's a slow night we stand a fair chance of not getting shot, robbed, or poisoned by the food."

In past lives, Butch's had been a Steak Pit, a Hamburger Palace, a Mexican restaurant, and quite possibly a drive-through bank. Artifacts of those lives—general layout, smell, signs and tiles, an extensive driveway system—lingered. A "piece" at Butch's turned out to be a quarter of a pie, and came on a dinner plate. Coffee arrived in cups the size of soup bowls. Probably did killer business once the bars skirting the edge of town shut down for the night. Which wasn't too far off, come to think of it.

He stirred milk into his coffee, looked at his piece of pie, and felt vaguely challenged by both. "Your father's a cop."

"One of *them*, yeah. And my mother was an illegal. He married her, made an honest woman of her. What does that make me?"

"Interesting?"

"Not really."

"Like your name then. Not interesting, you said before."

"When I was little, I climbed on everything. Chairs, trees, people's legs, toilets, cardboard boxes. Like a goat, my mother said. And Dad was Bill—"

"I get it."

"With an *-ie* to make it feminine."

Outside, two cars tried to pull into the parking lot at the same time. Both stopped. One driver got out, leaving the door open, and started toward the other car. That driver threw it in reverse, backed into the street, and floored it.

And just like that, for no good reason at all, he found himself telling Billie about his mother. How he'd sat chewing his Spam sandwich watching her go after his old man with a butcher knife and a bread knife, one ear on his plate and blood shooting out of the gash in his neck. How that was about it for the rest of her life, she'd used it all up.

"They were good knives, I hope," Billie said.

"Probably not, it was a cheap house. But they did their work."

"Her too."

"What do you mean?"

"Last thing she did, from what you say. A mother, protecting you."

Somehow that had never occurred to him. He always figured she'd just had enough.

"What's the story there?" Billie nodded to a booth where a fiftyish woman and a man in his twenties sat, she with eggs and bacon, he with salad. Was Billie picking up on his uneasiness, changing the subject in accord?

"Not mother and son," he said.

"And not lovers, the body language is all wrong."

"Yet they're both leaning in slightly."

"Dispensing and ignoring advice?"

"Confessing to one another, maybe." He braved the pie and for moments they were silent. The couple rose from the booth to leave by separate doors. "Law school, huh?"

"Second year."

"That's a longish walk from fixing people's cars."

"I don't know. How much of what we do in our lives, what we think, is chosen, and how much is just what comes at us? My dad was always fooling with cars, parking his on the street because some junker was getting fixed up in the garage. Same with my mother's cousins that came to live with us. Didn't have any money, and sent most of what they had back home, so they'd build these cars from spare parts and pieces. I'd watch them, and they'd hand me a wrench to pretend I was helping, and before long I was. Discovered I had a weird talent for it, like I could see how things were supposed to work, how they'd fit together, how much strength was needed here, how much relief there. At one point we had twelve people living in the house. Kids, cousins, hard to tell which were which. Mechanic's pay put me through undergrad, and I'll be out of ASU free and clear, no loans, nothing."

"And then?"

"Hard to say. See what turns up, I guess."

"What comes at you."

"Right."

"And if nothing does?"

"You never know. But it's not like I'll just be sitting around waiting, is it?"

He drank the rest of his coffee. There were grounds in the bottom of the cup. "You want another piece of pie? You could try the strawberry this time."

"I think this'll do me until about next March." She pushed the remains, crust, a smear of yellow, three tiny strands of coconut, toward him. "Have at it, big boy."

"Your father still a cop?"

"Some days more than others. But he hasn't worn the badge for almost ten years. He's in an assisted care facility full of nice retired shoe salesmen, dentists, and insurance brokers who keep trying to get him to play cards or checkers or some damn thing." She looked to the window outside which three Harleys (no mistaking the sound of them) cruised by in a rough V. "I kick in what his pension doesn't cover."

"And your mother?"

"Died three weeks after he hung the job up. And they had all these plans...." She leaned back against the half wall, legs stretched out on the booth's seat, cradling her coffee cup in both hands. "Don't we all."

A cook leaned forward to peer through the service slot from the kitchen, then came out and stood looking around, like a bus driver counting heads. He wore a green surgical scrub cap and was stick-thin except for a huge swell of belly.

"What about you?" Billie said.

"Plans? Not really." None he could talk about.

"That ride you're working on, that's just a lark? You can't be racing, or the guys would know you."

"I did race, down around Tucson, but that was long ago."

"You're not old enough to *have* a long ago, Eight."

"It's not always just years."

She met his eyes (beat-and-a-half, the director would say) and nodded.

They picked him up the next morning out by Globe. Two cars this time, and they'd waited for an isolated stretch of road. Chevy Caprice and a high-end Toyota. The message he sent back at the food court in the mall had been received.

He was working the Ford hard, letting it out, bringing it back in, slow, fast, slow again, learning its bounce and feed, but this was a little more testing than he anticipated.

The guy in front was good. Driver slowed enough to let him pass and he did, but then he let it ride, kept his distance. Knowing this wouldn't be an easy take down, and in no hurry.

The one in the rear car was there for good reason. A tightness to his steering. And he didn't hug his speed, he'd inch it up, fall back, whenever Driver picked up or dropped a few mphs.

Take him out first.

Driver slowed, started to speed, then slowed again and slammed the brakes. Watched the car behind try to stop and realize it couldn't. Watched it cut to the left and, knowing that's what he'd do, swung toward it. The car cut hard again to avoid collision and, losing its center, careened off the road, came within a hair's breadth of turning over, came back down on four wheels rocking. Out of the count for the while if not for good.

So Driver whipped a quick U and floored it, heading back toward lights, traffic, civilization.

Aggressors are like cats: they'll instinctively follow if you run. And that can give you the edge.

In the rearview he watched the lights of the lead car come around, watched them move in fast. Man had himself a good ride under that bland Chevy hood. Driver could hear the throatiness of the engine going full-out as it approached.

Been a long time since he'd done this, and he had to wonder if it would be there when he needed it. The instincts were good, but. And buts are what do you in.

The wall just ahead, he recalled from before. Earth color, like most everything else out here, with a sketchy lizard or cactus panel every few yards, the whole thing maybe 200 feet in length. Basically a sound baffle, houses, a small community, packed in beyond.

A median strip separated the lanes. There was fencing, but there were also gaps left for police, service vehicles and such. At the next gap, Driver turned hard, crossed the median and, with gravel spitting behind him, plunged into oncoming traffic. Not a lot of cars, but still dodgy. And horns aplenty. In the rearview mirror he saw his pursuer take down a stretch of fencing as he followed.

The wall, a couple of feet of packed ground, a low curb. If he could get the speed up, hit the curb just right...

Like that first gig back at the studio.

Driver cut left, coming in as straight as he could to the curb, then at the last moment hauled the wheels hard to the right. His head banged against the car's roof as he struck the curb—and he was *up*. The left wheels came back down, and came down rough, but on the wall, with the Ford running along at a fifty-degree tilt.

Then, as the Chevy closed in, Driver swung right again, bouncing back onto the highway and running full-tilt toward him. You haven't quite registered what's going on, you see a car rocketing toward you, you react. The Caprice slewed to the median, careened off the fencing and back onto the road, clipping a battered passenger car with its front end, a bright, new-looking van with its tail, as it spun.

Then everything got still, the way it does just before reload, and Driver was listening, listening for the sounds to start up. Slammed doors. Screams. Sirens.

He'd brought the Ford to a stop with a one-eighty down the road quite a ways, and now he looked back at the pile-up as though well apart from it all, an observer just come upon the scene. There would be injured. And very soon there would be police. Police and cameras and questions.

Driver closed his eyes to focus on heart rate and breathing, slow long intake. Battlefield breathing: five in, hold five, five out. As he opened his eyes, a black van was pulling in behind him. The driver stayed inside. The passenger got out, held up his hands palm outward, grew slowly larger in the rearview mirror as he approached. Grey suit, thirtyish, short-cut hair, walk and bearing suggesting military, athlete, both.

Driver rolled down his window.

The man kept his distance. "Mr. Beil says hello."

"He was having me followed?"

"Actually, we were watching them." He nodded toward the Chevy. "That one, and his friend you left up the road." He looked off a moment to the west. Moments later, Driver heard the sirens. "Cell phones. Never give you much time these days. Leave now. We've got it."

"People in the other cars could be seriously injured."

"We'll do this. Check them all, get those who need it to the hospital and make sure they get the best care, talk to them, eyewitness the cops. When we clean, we clean everything." His smile was the width of a line of light showing under a snugly fit door. "It's a package deal." The man nodded. The nod was about the same girth as the smile. "You'll be wanting to give Mr. Beil a call, first chance you get."

"Opinions are like assholes," Shannon used to say, "everybody has one. But convictions, that's a different horse—convictions are more dangerous enemies of truth than lies."

That last was from Nietzsche, though Driver didn't know it at the time. These past years, Driver had caught up on a lot of things. He didn't think Shannon believed in any kind of truth that you could put in a box and take home with you. But he definitely knew his way around lies. The lies that are told to us from birth, the ones we're swimming in, the ones we tell ourselves in order to go on.

He'd left the Fairlane parked by the garage and, with no home temporary or otherwise to return to, found a motel up toward town. The clerk, who kept patting at his hair with flat fingers, made him wait in a smelly lobby chair with burn holes (Driver counted sixteen in the hour he waited) because it wasn't check-in time. The room was everything the chair promised.

He turned on the TV, which didn't work, and turned it off. What the hell, he could hear the one from the adjoining room perfectly anyway. The stains in the toilet bowl and tub were a world to themselves. When he sat on it, the bed made a sound that reminded him of buckboards in old westerns.

But he needed rest, he was going to have a shitload of work to do tomorrow to get the car back up, and this was as good a place as any to go to ground. No one would find him, no one would look for him here.

He believed that right up until he came awake to the sound of his room door closing.

The intruder would stand there for a time, of course. Not moving, hardly breathing, listening. That's how it was done. Driver coughed lightly, a half cough, the way we do when sleeping, and turned on his side, made to be settling back in.

One tentative footstep, a pause, then another. A couple of people went by just outside, stepping hard and talking, causing Driver to narrow his focus. The intruder would ride that noise, use it to cover his approach.

Don't think, *act*, as Shannon had told him over and over. Driver never really saw or heard the man—sensed him more than anything—and was off the bed at a roll, able to make out the man's form now, the outline of it against window light, striking out with his elbow at where the man's face should be, feeling and hearing the crunch of bone.

Driver had his foot on the man's throat by the time he was down, but he wasn't going to be getting up anytime soon. Driver grabbed a towel from the bathroom and dropped it by him, then sat on the floor nearby, opening his pocket knife and holding it so that would be the first thing the man saw when he came around.

It didn't take long. His eyes opened, swam a bit before they cleared, went to Driver. He turned his head to spit out blood. Looked back and waited.

"From around here?" Driver asked.

"Dallas."

Imported talent, then. Interesting. He put away the knife. "What about the others?"

"I don't know anything about any others, man."

"What *do* you know?"

"I know there was five large waiting for me once I walked out of here."

"But you're not walking out, are you."

"There is that."

"You want to see Texas again?"

The man licked his lips, tasting blood. He put two fingers up and lightly touched his ruined nose. "That would be the most agreeable outcome, yes."

"Then let's get you in a chair and talk."

"About?"

"How you're getting paid, where, who. That sort of thing."

Driver helped him up. Blood streamed from his face once the man was upright. He held the towel to his nose, speaking through it. "You know you can't outrun this, right? When I'm gone, there'll be someone else."

So for the moment this was what it came down to, perched with a failed killer at world's edge in the middle of the night, thinking about convictions. Had he ever had any? And what kind of lies was he telling himself, to think he might somehow find a way through all this?

He'd driven back out Van Buren to Sky Harbor, had his night visitor call from the airport to tell them it was done. Stopped at a dollar store on the way to get the man a new shirt and slacks. No way TSA was letting him through with blood all over him.

The pickup was in Glendale. Driver headed that way and parked up the street from All-Nite Diner, the only thing left alive in a three- or four-block radius, the rest given over equally to retail stores and offices. The diner itself was shared by two cops and, judging from their hats and Western finery, members of The Biscuit Band, whose van sat out front. Mail N More, halfway up the block and in easy view, opened in a little over an hour. Driver bought a carry-out coffee and went back to the car to wait. He passed the time perusing windows. Those at Mail N More read:

Boxes for rent	Money Orders	Photocopies
Will Call Service	Messengering	Packaging
Notary Inside	Business cards	Habla Espanol

The window at the antique store across the street read, THEY DON'T MAKE LIFE LIKE THEY USED TO.

He was thinking about these people who kept coming after him. They bring in hired help, it suggests what? That they're limited, maybe a small group working on their own? Which didn't make much sense, given the professionalism of the strikes—their own people came in first, he had to assume—not to mention Beil's presence in this. Because they wanted to maintain distance, deniability? Or they were running out of soldiers?

Yeah, right.

At 7:54 a dark brown Saturn pulled up in front of Mail N More. The driver turned off his engine and sat. When the card hanging inside the door flipped to OPEN, he got out and went in, carrying an 11x13 padded envelope. Youngish guy, black, late twenties, dark suit, white shirt, no tie. He handed the envelope to the man at the desk, took out his wallet, paid him. When he came back out, Driver was sitting behind the Saturn's wheel.

"What, I forgot to lock it?"

"Phoenix does rate pretty high in car theft."

"You want to come out from there?"

"Why don't you join me instead? We can talk privately."

Driver watched the man's eyes check sidewalk, streets, and diner. The police car had pulled away minutes earlier. The diner was filling with people on their way to work. Driver reached under the dash, twisted together the wires he'd pulled down before. The engine came to life.

"Another minute, I drive away. You get in, I stay."

The man came around to the passenger side, opened the door and stood with his hand on it. "This is decidedly not smart," he said.

"I get dumber every year."

The man climbed in, and Driver killed the engine.

"So dumb," Driver said, "that I don't care about the money you just left in there."

He looked at Driver, looked back out to the street. "Yeah, okay."

"What I do care about is knowing who it came from."

"Why?"

"Knowledge makes us a better person, don't you think?"

"No," he said. "No, I don't. Don't think that at all. Four years polishing college chairs with my bottom, three more of law school, and I end up a gopher. There's your knowledge."

"At some point you made the choice."

"Choices, yeah, that's what it's all about, isn't it? Free will, the common good. Still have my class notes somewhere."

"Choices don't have to be forever."

The man turned back to him. "You just get off a guest spot with Oprah, or what?"

They sat watching a white-haired oldster chug down the street in a golf cart at fifteen mph. He had a tiny American flag flying from an antenna at one corner, a dozen or more bumper stickers plastered all along the cart's sides.

"The money?" Driver said.

"You know I can't tell you that."

"Knowledge again." Driver put both hands in plain view on the steering wheel. "Then I'm afraid you won't be leaving this car."

"You think you can do that?"

"Where I live, it happens in a minute. A minute later the do-er's grabbing a sandwich."

The oldster pulled up by Mail N More. He took a plastic grocery bag out of his back pocket and snapped it open, went in. Came out with what looked to be only a few pieces of mail in the bag.

"Probably the high point of his day."

"Perspective is everything," Driver said.

"Yeah."

They sat watching the golf cart make its way back along the street, cars stacking up behind.

"I finished school, top ten percent of my class, had it made. All these firms on campus looking for talent, gladhanding me. Grabbed at the job when a top firm offered. There's like three chiefs and two hundred

Indians, every one of them in the top ten percent, every one of them scary smart. Turns out the firm hadn't hired another Indian, they'd just bought themselves a new horse."

Driver was silent.

"The corral's on Highland, near 24th Avenue. Genneman, Brewer, and Sims. This particular errand came from Joseph Brewer's assistant, Tim. Yellow hair. Not blond, yellow. And clothes just a little too tight. That's what I know." The cart turned eastward off the street four blocks up. "For the record: I made the delivery. I leave, reboot at the office, everything's square."

"And no one knows about our conversation."

"My point."

"As I said, it was private."

Driver got out, watched the Saturn as it pulled away. He found himself thinking of the man, not much younger than he was, actually, as a kid. What was that phrase Manny used? *Spilled anew into the world.* A new horse, the kid had said. Ridden—he was definitely ridden.

Joseph Brewer's assistant, Tim Bresh, lived in one of the enclaves near Encanto Park, a jumble of old Craftsman homes and carport suburbans from the fifties. Half the Craftsmans looked trashed, half of them gussied up and gentrified. Lots of For Sale signs out front of both. Bresh's sat between a long-unpainted wooden house all but invisible behind a screen of oleanders, and another of slump block painted such a vivid white that it looked unreal, not of this world. Bresh's was off-white, ivory maybe, but where mowers and ground water and time had nibbled at borders, patches of aqua showed.

Having posed as a messenger with a sign-for package addressed to Joseph Brewer, Driver had bluffed his way into the upper digestive tract of Genneman, Brewer, and Sims, to the outer office of Brewer himself and there tagged Bresh, yellow hair and all. The package, not that it mattered, contained a book, the latest full-tilt indictment of pyramid-scheme capitalism and those who fed off it. Driver liked to imagine Brewer picking up the book repeatedly, puzzling over its source and message. Realistically, he knew the bastard had probably just tossed it in the shredder. Or had his assistant do so.

"I'll get it," someone said from inside when Driver hit the bell.

A woman opened the door. Tall, halter top, shorts, thin arms—*spindly* came to mind. Her hair was wet, from a shower, from swimming. She and Driver stood listening as the intro to "Sympathy for the Devil" faded.

"Gets me every time," the woman said.

"That's quite a doorbell. Is Tim—"

But there Tim was, stepping up behind her. In his hand he had what looked to be a brandy snifter filled with what smelled to be Bailey's. He stared a moment.

"Don't I know you?"

Then he had it.

"The package. That book, *Street Smarts*, with the S made of dollar signs. Cute. I'm sure Joe's home wading into the thick of it as we speak, just his sort of thing." He stopped, as though taking a minute to wonder what Driver's sort of thing might be. Hard to say what was showing in his face. Wariness? Speculation?

"What can I do for you?" he said. "You don't seem to be making a delivery."

"Carry-out this time." Driver had edged into the room.

"Okay."

"Maybe your friend should leave."

"Or you should."

Driver shook his head.

"Look." Bresh moved farther inside, to allow him more room. "GBS has eighteen lawyers, not to mention paralegals, secretaries, and the usual office trash. That's a lot of personalities, a lot of egos—even without the clients, who, given the firm's fees, tend to be a demanding lot. And who do you think keeps the thing running? Me. So, same as I say day after day, just tell me what you want."

"One of your lawyers made a drop out in Glendale early this morning. Black, late twenties, driving a Saturn."

"I can't—"

"I know what he dropped, and why. I need to know who made the call, who sent him. Your name floated to the top."

"I see. And you need to know this because?"

Driver didn't answer right away. Finally he said, "Because I'm here and asking quietly."

"You followed me."

Driver nodded. He saw in Bresh's eyes that he had it all, the fake delivery, the tag, all of it.

"It wasn't me," Bresh said. "I called Donnie, sure, passed the message along. That's what I do mostly. It's a big place, GBS."

The woman nodded, though it was more of a bob. "Huge. It just kinda goes on and on."

"You work there too?"

"Computer geek. Timmy thinks *he* runs the show. I'm the one who really does."

"You know those guys you always see in the mall and so on," Bresh said, "old guys with bowling pin heads, a big round belly, and pipestem legs sticking out the bottom? That's what GBS is like, only under the round belly there's like a hundred legs, all of them going in different directions."

"Now's when Timmy usually breaks into his rogue bulldozer speech. Hope you're not in a hurry."

"You ever read Weber?" Bresh went on. "About bureaucracies? Firms like GBS, that's what they came down to long ago. It's all about not losing one's seat on the bus, all about keeping the machine running the way it always has. Everything else—clients, employees, law itself—is secondary."

"Doesn't sound much like your loyalty oath took."

"I'm part of the machine—"

"I *am* the bulldozer!" his friend said.

"—but that doesn't mean I can't see it."

Bresh put his drink down on the narrow table just inside the door. Its far end was taken up by a transparent blue vase of silk flowers, cattails, and feather fans on long handles. In the center sat a wicker basket heaped with milky-white crystal eggs not much larger than marbles.

"There's a man kept on retainer who does work for the company from time to time. Supposedly a messenger service, that's how it's billed, though there's no listing for such anywhere I've looked."

"What kind of work?"

"Can't really say. Doesn't happen in my yard. He liaisons with a junior partner."

"And that's where the call, your call, came from? To send the money out with Donnie?"

Bresh nodded. "Richard Cole, that's who you want to talk to. You can catch him at the office tomorrow, follow *him* home. Or—" He picked the drink up again and turned toward what was presumably the kitchen, speaking as he went. "Or I could just give you his address."

"Don't care for cards, do you?"

Bill didn't look at him. Another goddamned beautiful day outside the window. The window, of course, was sealed.

"Or TV. Or much of anything 'round here, you come right down to it. Am I right?"

Wendell turned back from the blinds he'd opened. Sunlight fell like a sloppy drunk across the floor.

"'S all about choices, Mr. Bill. I can choose not to be a crackhead dog like my mother was. You can choose not to lay up in there like a man who's dying when we both know you're not. Not hardly."

Wendell laughed. Lot of chest in that laugh.

"Choices. Listen to me, I sound like one of the social workers always giving ol' mom their good advice. Not to mention, a few of 'em, six or ten inches of hard dick."

Despite himself, Bill laughed.

"There it is. Not something dead and dying men do a lot, laugh. Good thing, too. You imagine how noisy graveyards would get to be?"

Bill sat on the edge of the bed. Wendell was handing him his shoes. Rubbed at the tops with his shirt sleeve as he did so.

"Tell you what. 'Bout ten minutes, they're gonna be starting up a gospel singalong out there in the day room. I saw the choir members when they got off the bus, be one hell of a racket made. And I'm not much more of a mind to sit through that than you are. What say you and me go for a walk? Get good earth under our feet."

B ack his first year in town, he and Shannon were on the set of *Doomtown Days*, a post-apocalypse film. Studios were turning out a lot of them then, mostly on shoestring budgets. Reluctantly heroic, barely dressed man or woman stalking across the wasteland alone, communities gone feral, automotive equivalents of zip guns, zombie sheep, that sort of thing.

Shannon had just said that the director looked to be all of sixteen years old. "Kid musta clipped out an ad from the back of a comic book. *Want to direct movies?* Sent in his two dollars."

There was a guy hanging around the edges, wearing a print shirt, creased high-pocket trousers. Neither young nor old, good-looking or plain, nothing to draw attention to him. Driver pointed, asked who's that?

"Danny Louvin. Everything you see here goes back to him."

Driver looked again. Put a Your-Name-Here ID bracelet on him, a puka-shell necklace, he'd win the award for uncool. "That's the money man?"

"The money man's sitting over there in the producer tent. Knit shirt, leather loafers? Danny's the one who keeps it running, makes it all work."

"He doesn't seem to be doing anything."

"That's how good he is."

Driver remembered that as he drove out Cave Creek Road. Clump after clump of housing developments squatted on what within easy memory had been bare desert. He wondered if, late afternoons, the coyotes still came out, and what they must think about all this. Dark swatches showed on the hills where clouds blocked sunlight, making the landscape look like parts from two different worlds hastily patched together.

He was thinking about the people you see and the ones you don't, the ones who really run things. Take this too far, it blooms to paranoia, you start finding conspiracies in how cereal boxes get lined up on the shelf. Consider it too little, you're a fool.

Bresh believed that he ran the office at GBS, he was the one who kept things together. Maybe he was. And what about Beil, who claimed to be merely a broker, an arranger, a middleman? How far did *his* influence extend? Was there a wizard for every curtain? Or just one, behind all the curtains?

Billboards advertising a new community under construction out this way showed a string of faces from infant to elderly and read *The Better Life You've Been Looking For*. Driver remembered something else

Shannon had told him, the story of a traveller who gave his life because he wanted to visit a town that was like all others in its area, but forbidden. He remembered it because the writer had been there when Shannon told the story. Two days later that same situation showed up in the ongoing rewrite of the script.

Richard Cole's home was green stucco and had fake logs or at least fake stubs of logs built high into the outside walls. Plastic barn owls stood at each corner of the roof, searching the skies. Two cars in the driveway, a midnight blue Lexus and a red two-seater BMW.

No door bell, but a knocker shaped like a bear's head. Driver used it then stepped aside, to the edge of the peephole's sweep, turning to look away, as if in appreciation of the landscape.

"Who is it?" came from inside.

Driver didn't respond. After a moment the door started open. Driver waited. When it was fully open, and the man stood there, anger and presumption spilling off his face, Driver took a single step forward and hit him once, hard as he could, directly in the forehead. Watched him stagger back and go down, saw the other guy come up from the couch.

"Bad idea," Driver said.

The guy sat down. The two of them were dressed almost like twins, loose-fitting tan slacks, blue broadcloth shirts, soft, costly leather slip-ons. As Cole got back to his feet, this one slid furtively down to reach for the cell phone in what had been designed a century ago as a watch pocket.

"Worse idea," Driver said. The guy held up both hands, palms out.

Cole looked at his friend, made a disgusted face, and looked back. His forehead was turning dark. "Who are you?"

"A delivery boy. Like Donnie."

No response.

"Donnie—who, at your urging, carried a padded envelope into Mail N More this morning?"

Still nothing.

"What you're going to tell me is where *your* urge came from."

"Get out of my house."

Driver turned as if to go, then spun back, right foot hooking Cole's knee, pulling his legs out from under him. The man went down with a loud crack that probably heralded concussion. Driver planted the foot on his stomach.

"Please," Driver said.

Cole didn't try to move, but his eyes were going everywhere, north, south, east, west. White ceiling. Beige walls. Furniture legs. Ivory carpet. His friend's feet showing beneath the couch. None of it any help.

That's how suddenly the world you were sure you understood can change, Driver thought.

Cities were so various, they wore so many different faces. Leaving the easy, spare opulence of Cave Creek and Carefree behind, he drove in past Deer Valley Road and the federal prison to the dry-stalk stretches of outer Phoenix, and it was as though he drove through not one but half a dozen cities stacked beside and atop one another. Churches had re-upped as tax offices. A huge store and lot once given over to selling farm machinery was now a swap meet. The Dairy Queen, nothing changed but the sign, had become Mariscos Juarez.

Turn left at a gated community, two blocks away people are hauling mattresses down outside stairs and cooking on driveways in vats the size of cannibal pots.

Darkness was well on its way, spreading its hand flat against the city, as he drove back in. Billie had offered her uncle's place to him. "For as long as you need it," she'd said, Uncle Clayton currently residing several thousand miles away "helping repair some of the damage we'd done earlier," whatever that meant. She's saying for as long as you need it, but he's thinking until they find me there, and declined. So he was at an extended-stay hotel two blocks up and another over, a knight's move, from Colter and Twelfth. One room with a single entrance and the windows bolted shut, but they weren't anymore. And he had full view of the approach, driveway, parking lot.

He also had a diner across the street, where he and Billie were meeting. Enough red—roof outside, booth covering, tiles, seats at the counter, aprons, napkins—to send you away color blind, but good, cheap food. Waitresses, like the diner itself, looked to be from the fifties. They took your order, stepped away, turned and came back with your food, that's how it felt.

Billie had come directly from the garage in work clothes and boots, grease under her nails, a Nike swoosh of it down one cheek. Everyone in the diner gave the impression of having barely arrived from one place while being eager to depart for another. Feet fidgeted under tables. Eyes swung toward windows.

Not just here, Driver told himself. The whole world's like that now.

He remembered standing over Bernie Rose's body in L.A., there at frontier's end, as Bernie's final breath hissed out. Remembered getting back in the stripped-down Datsun, feeling comforted by its throb, thinking that he drove, that was what he did, that was what he'd always do.

"Interesting group," Billie said. "Starting with the waitresses' costumes."

"If you mean the hair and all, I don't think that's a costume."

"Uh-huh. And the cook?" Periodically his head had appeared in the gunwale through which plates passed from kitchen to servers. Thin hair parted severely at the side, nose that seemed to be drawing the face relentlessly forward. "Too many black and white movies?"

Just then a group of five, mixed men and women, came in from some affair or another, made out as zombies. Torn clothes, pasty white faces, blackened eyes, splatters of food color, beads of drool. All of them staggered about, arms flailing as though subject to a different musculature, a different gravity. They took a corner booth, where one of them began quietly to chant *Flesh! Flesh!*

Driver was halfway through his Breakfast-Any-Time. He put his fork down and said, "I need to tell you something."

"Wondered when you'd get to it."

"That obvious, huh?"

"Not really."

"But?"

She shrugged.

"Fair enough."

And he told her. Not so much about the older life, just the bare bones of that. But about how he had stood over Elsa's body, how in the past he had killed, again and again. How killers were now coming for him. How they kept coming, might well keep coming for the rest of his life. How short that *rest* might be.

When he stopped talking, she looked away, then back at him.

"They're eating salads," she said. "The zombies." She popped in the last bite of burger. "So in other words, you find yourself unaccountably pursued—fatally, you assume—by unapprehended forces."

"Those are definitely other words. But yeah, that's pretty much it. Hard to believe?"

"No, I'm just sitting here wondering what my philosophy teacher would have to say. Dark room, dark hat. Shoulder to the door against an unseen, silent, unknown resistance. An interesting man. 'Actuality is something brute,' he'd tell us. 'There is no reason in it.' Yet everything in his own life, how he talked, how he taught, the way he dressed, seemed nailed to logic's door."

Billie smiled up as the waitress refilled her coffee. Looking back to him, Billie's eyes dropped to the waitress' name tag. "Thanks, JoAnne." Then, as JoAnne moved on: "What *I'm* thinking is, you could use some help with this."

Late morning, Raymond Phelps was half asleep in the reclining lawn chair on his patio, half thinking about where to grab lunch, Thai maybe, or one of those crushed grilled sandwiches at the Cuban place. Something took his attention, woke him. A sound, insect, hunger. Something.

When he opened his eyes a face hovered upside down above his.

"You don't want to be moving," the face said.

And when he did, a hammer struck him full force in the belly.

"That's why you don't want to." The hammer and the hand holding it came into view. "Found this over by the wall. A long time ago you must have cared, worked at trying to keep things shipshape. Now just look at it. Rust, handle rotting. How much can you tell about a man from his tools, Ray?"

"Who the fuck—"

The hammer struck again before he could finish. He vomited, coffee, juice and stomach acids searing his throat.

The man waited till he was done.

"Eight inches to either side, you've got gravel for a hip. Ten inches south…"

"What do you want?"

"I want you to understand that this is not going to be a conversation. I'll ask questions. You'll answer. Briefly, directly."

Raymond started to lift a hand to wipe his mouth, stopped and looked back at the man.

"Go ahead." Again, he waited. "We're good?"

Raymond nodded.

"Two days ago you called Richard Cole, had him arrange for a money drop out in Glendale."

Raymond nodded. More coffee, juice and acid was at the gate.

"That money was to pay talent brought in from Dallas."

"Yes."

"Who was the hit on?'

"I'm guessing you know that." He vomited again, but all that came up were some strings of thin, gluey fluid.

"Did you have a photo?"

"A description. Vehicle. Probable locations."

"Who placed the order?"

Raymond started to talk, stopped when he thought he was going to vomit but managed to swallow it down. "Can we go inside?"

The man stood from his crouch, waving the hammer toward the patio door.

The office inside was everything Raymond wasn't: well appointed, orderly, efficient, clean. Metal shelving covered two walls, folders aligned and held in place by letter boxes, numbers on the shelves, index tabs protruding along the bottom of the folders here and there. Glancing into the kitchen beyond—smeared counters, greasy stovetop, ragtag piles of dishes—Driver was newly astonished at the contrast.

He looked back at the shelves.

"This is what the world looked like before computers took over."

"Computer files, yeah. Easy to copy, easy to erase. And I have duplicates of all this hidden away."

"Insurance?"

"Insurance, memory, archives. Whatever word suits you."

Raymond pointed questioningly to the shelves. When Driver nodded, he walked over and plucked a folder. No scanning, no hesitation. Went right to it. Brought it back and handed it over.

Driver flipped it open. Email transcripts. Account records and financial paperwork. Reports from credit agencies, a Better Business Bureau, a licensing organization. Photocopies of handwritten notes that looked to have originated in a daybook or pocket notebook. Membership lists.

"Won't take you there, but it's a map."

"Not someone you've worked with before, then."

"And a lot of blinds. I always look in the water, deep as I can. Same as you, I'm sure. Near as I can make out, this one came by way of a lawyer in or around New Orleans."

"No idea who's behind it?"

"Someone with a shitload of money." Raymond held out his hand for the folder. "Give me a minute. I'll run copies."

"There's a couple old running buddies down that way I could send round."

"Tattoos may not work here, Felix."

"Doyle's will. *Semper Fi.* And the leg's prosthetic. Heartbreaker of a limp when he wants. The one that'll be with him…Never says much, but he asks a question, you're just naturally inclined to answer."

"Sounds good."

"I'll get them on it, get back to you when."

"Care, my friend."

"I'll take it."

Billie had her head on the seat, eyes closed, when he climbed back in the car. They'd tried multiple places. Now they were out behind a long-closed bowling alley on its way to becoming a flea market and swap mart. Workers were grinding down pink stucco with belt sanders.

"Your friend always that hard to find?"

"Until he knows who's looking."

"Ever think about trying a phone?"

"He's more a face-to-face guy."

"In-your-face from the look."

"It's happened."

She had a rubber band in her teeth as she pulled her hair back. Talked around it, then slipped the hair through. "Any butts you need to kick for the next hour or so?"

"It can wait. You had something in mind?"

"I was going to see my father, thought maybe you'd come along."

Willow Villa was in a stretch of commercial property that sprang up unannounced. One minute they were cruising past ranch houses and shrubs and double driveways, then signs were all around them. *Bernard Capes, Chiropractor. Action Limbs and Prosthetics. Spine Mechanics. Physical Therapy Associates.* As though some weird medical mall had claimed squatter's rights and was taking form before your eyes.

Two cars in the visitor's parking lot around back, one of them a 1968 Pontiac GTO that could have just come off the showroom floor. Driver and Billie watched as seven elderly ladies came out of the building, spent at least three minutes getting into the car, and drove slowly down the drive, hitting the street with a dip and loud clang.

Inside, they stopped to sign in. The air was cold and stale and smelled vaguely of raw alcohol. Two women sat at desks beyond the counter. One had an account or records book of some kind. The other was peering at a computer screen, and looked up. Her hair was three different colors, none of them natural, none of them, for that matter, found in nature.

"Hey, Billie."

"Maxine. You're back."

"As of yesterday."

"Your son's better, then?"

"For now....Mr. Bill's not in his room, honey."

"Oh?"

"Out for a walk with Wendell, can you believe it? Getting to be a regular thing."

"Which way?"

She pointed to the back of the building.

"Max always thought the boy just had asthma," Billie said as they went back through the doors. "Two weeks ago he had a crisis, two o'clock in the morning the way it usually happens, and they wound up in ER at Good Sam. Came to find out it's a heart defect, something that should have been caught years ago. There they are."

Driver and Billie walked toward two men sitting at a plastic patio table. A scruffy Chinese elm struggled to give shade.

"Hi, Daddy, I thought you were out walking."

The older man looked for a moment at Driver before answering.

Cop's look, Driver thought.

"Wendell got tired."

"Of course he did."

"Wendell, you know my daughter. And she's brought a friend. This," he said, looking again at Driver, then at Wendell, "is *my* friend."

"Pleased to meet you, sir. Miss Billie." Wendell stood. Scars and a Special Forces tattoo intertwined with cords of muscle on his arms. "I'd best be getting back. You okay out here, Mr. Bill?"

Billie's father nodded. Driver and Billie sat at the table. Off ten or twelve yards, where a path led to a stand of trees, a cat repeatedly scampered and leapt, twisting about in midair, as it stalked a huge Viceroy butterfly.

"Good to see you out here, Dad. This is Eight—long story, don't ask. We work together."

Both he and Driver were watching the cat. "Pleased to meet you, sir."

Billie waited. "I'm afraid my father doesn't have much to say these days."

He turned back, looked at Driver.

"So you work with my girl. Not another damn lawyer, are you, like the last one?"

"No, sir. No, I'm not."

"Not a lawyer? Or not like the last one?"

"Both."

"And you got a number for a name, like in that Merle Haggard song."

"Courtesy of your daughter, yes, sir."

"Always did see things the way *she* wanted to. And that's one of her *good* points."

"We're the descendents of the ones who ran—and of the ones who fought. You just gotta figure out when to what." Felix looked up the alleyway. "Help soon be on the way in their pretty squads. Don't think you'll be wanting to take time to check out."

They went over the wall together, into the lot of a quickie car service long closed down. Someone, kids most likely, had piled up a bunch of used tires back here and set them afire. Been a while, but the smell had moved in to stay.

"That does bring back memories," Felix said, looking at the mound. "Your ride?"

"Over by Food City."

They walked that way.

Half an hour ago Driver had returned to his room to find that things were not as he left them. Did their best to keep it from showing, but they'd been in the drawers where clothes had been refolded, his razor and toothbrush were out of place by an inch, and there was a faint odor, like an aftertaste, of sweet cologne. The smell's what tipped him.

He went downstairs to the front desk. A stocky twentyish woman was on duty, her arms so thickly tattooed that she seemed to be wearing comic books for sleeves. She looked up. "Room got messed with, huh?"

He nodded.

"Dark blue sedan parked 'round back. Police, or claim to be."

"See a badge?"

"You mean like the one I could buy off the street for the price of a cup of highlife coffee?"

When Driver pointed to the doorway leading back to storage and services, she nodded.

"No one back there?"

"Rarely."

Minutes later Driver exited the rear door onto the parking lot pushing a steel cart piled with everything heavy he could find. Nested metal trashcans, five cinder blocks, a footlocker, an unopened box of footlong rebar. He made as though to go left, toward the dumpsters. Both heads in the blue sedan swivelled to look, then turned back. When they did, Driver broke to a run, slamming the cart into the sedan so hard that he all but fell from the rebound. The passenger door buckled. The man on his side couldn't get out. The other one came at him over the top of the car.

Driver pulled the cart back, caught the man between it and the car as he clambered down. The other one was out of the car now too, but that had to wait. Driver pulled the cart back, slammed it again into the man. Then again. And again. Till he heard a voice.

"Think we're done here, friend."

When Driver pulled the cart back, his man fell. Blood snailed from his mouth. His legs twitched.

Felix stood over the other one. "Heard the commotion back this way, occurred to me you might not be far off."

Just before they'd gone over the wall, an elderly security guard had stepped around from the front of the building carrying a walkie-talkie. Seeing the wreck and the two on the ground, he'd stopped, raised both hands over his head, and quick-stepped back the way he came.

Now they were crossing the street to Food City. A Gran Torino, expertly streeted out and bearing a sprawl of exotic birds and equally exotic women painted in metallic blues and yellows pulled up at the light, bass pounding such that Driver and Felix could feel it coming up their legs from the pavement. The battered Toyota next to it had Rochelle, Juan, and Stephanie painted in script on the rear window, with tiny crosses beneath each.

"Still hanging in with the ride, anyway," Felix said as they approached the Fairlane. "Even if you can't seem to hold on to a residence for shit."

As they walked, Felix told him what he'd come to tell him, before what he called that little mash-up in the parking lot.

"Doyle was on his best behavior, even made an appointment. Went limping in on time and took his seat politely in the waiting area. Plastic that looked like leather, he said, stuck to your skin, crackled every time you moved. Woodreau and Levin, Attorneys at Law. Out in Metairie. Lore was with him. Pretending to read a book, Doyle said, you shoulda seen it. Receptionist kept looking over at him.

"Doyle gets back there and it's some kid, looks like he's sixteen. An associate, he says. 'Didn't come all this way to talk to an associate,' Doyle tells him. 'I assure you,' the kid begins, and Doyle stops him. 'Why don't you save us both some worry and go bring back a grown man?'

"He does, and Doyle apologizes, tells this grown man how sometime when his leg gets to hurting he just turns a little cranky, you know? Asks the man if he served and the man says yes. 'Navy?' Doyle says, 'you got that look about you.' Man nods and asks how he can be of help."

Felix had stopped at that point and said, "Amazing what simple courtesy can accomplish."

"Absolutely. The Marine way."

"Took him less than thirty minutes. And with only a *little* insistence. Didn't even have to call in Lore, boy stayed out there pretending to read his book and smiling back at the receptionist whenever she'd look his way.

"Lawyers were blind. You knew that. Brokers, as Mr. Levin himself put it, to which Doyle responded that broke-ing was something he got forced to do as well, upon occasion. That, he said, had Mr. L's attention.

"It was at that point that Mr. L thought it wise to call security and Doyle disagreed to such extent that Mr. L's hand is now in a cast. Doyle was thinking maybe he should drop by again, be the first to sign it."

"Probably not."

"Yeah, probably."

Someone behind them had said excuse me and when they turned, parting, two middle-aged men in shorts and sandals stepped between them. One held aloft a whitewashed cross, the other a four-foot wooden sword.

"There goes the human race and its entire history in a nutshell," Felix said. He and Driver turned under the overpass and walked on.

"Doyle wants you to know how tracking this guy resembled looking for one specific snake in the Atchafalaya swamp."

"But he did it."

"Your man's a cipher," Felix said. "A businessman, one of those whose footprint shows up all over the place. Owns a car dealership, a theater or two, a chain of sporting goods stores, an import company, high-end wine shops, a dozen others. No trouble with the law, half a dozen court cases in civil court, mostly settled, no hands across the sea or across a checkered tablecloth with Sinatra singing. No apparent connection to you. Gerald Dunaway."

"And he's the one who wants to shut me down?"

Felix nodded. "That's where it starts. One step off Dunaway's porch, though, and riders start showing up."

"Hired help."

"Maybe just that. Hitchhikers, pilot fish. Or could be shared interests, whatever they might be. Alliances, coalitions, all those gentrified, uptown words for gangs. Doyle's still poking at the anthill."

They were at the car now. The door hadn't fit right or worked well since the set-to with the Chevy Caprice and Toyota out by Globe. Driver kept meaning to fix it. He'd done the essential engine and suspension resets but let the body work hang. When he pulled the door open, it made a sound like swords coming out of scabbards in bad fantasy movies.

"Nice," Felix said. "Distinctive." He ran his hand along the door's edge. "Interesting thing about this Dunaway is how he came into the money, the bulk of it anyway. Doyle has a friend, a service buddy, who works in the sheriff's office over in Jefferson Parish. Says Dunaway's one of those who lived uptown, stuck it out through Katrina. And afterwards, right after, he made a fortune or three selling food and water to the un- and re-located. No one knows where the food and water came from for sure, but rumors have them as diverted relief and humanitarian goods. After *that*, he started buying up huge sections of the city for pennies—all of this paper-legal, of course."

"Sounds like carpetbaggers."

"What I said. Doyle claims that New Orleans grows its own, always has. No need to bus them in."

"This Dunaway married? Family? Children?"

"Wife died in 1998, accidental death according to official reports, suicide according to some unofficial ones. No one else we can tag."

"He's a native?"

"In the city since 1988. Brooklyn before that. Like I said, Doyle's still tapping at it. And he taps good."

"It's in our nature—in our bones, our spleen, our amygdyla, or wherever we've gone to locating the ineffable this year—to try to connect the dots," Manny said. "Just as it is to go rummaging around in the dark for that one idea that explains *everything*. Economics. Religion. Conspiracy. String theory."

Driver had punched in the number fitfully, a back-wash of sadness finding him as he did so. It was a feeling he had experienced before, this sense of doing something for the last time. You never knew its source.

"Things happen. They don't have to add up to more. Hang on."

Not that one, Driver heard him say. The bottle shaped like a fencepost, with the fake knotholes.

"Got a producer here. Grand plans and a budget to match. All he needs is a script. We're dipping into the good stuff I save for special occasions."

"The good stuff is in a bottle with knotholes?"

"Okay, they're aesthetically challenged. But at what they do…"

Driver heard Manny take a sip, imagining palate and mood slowly changing color, rust to peach to pink, like that. Then he was back.

"Let's run it down. Storyboard it. First you have this guy in NoLa. Dunaway. No doubt about what he's in it for, you say."

"Right."

"But you don't know why."

"Again."

"Different music, different lighting, late night with rain maybe, this Beil character turns up. Has a guardian angel or two sicced on you. And tries his best to press-gang you onto his ship. To fight for the common good, common bad, whatever. Next, a couple more get dropped in, these troopers that Beil's men were shadowing. The guy at the mall, too? No idea where *they* hang hats. Makes for a thick soup, my friend. Any others in the cooker?"

"We'll see, won't we?"

"Only if you live long enough."

Manny took another sip. Driver could hear the producer talking there at the other end, wondered whether Manny was ignoring him or managing to carry on both conversations.

"Do the dots connect? Could be all random. Separate storms. And in the long run what does it matter? The question's always the same: What do you do? How do you act? Hold on, I'm going out to the patio."

Moments later, against a faint backdrop of traffic sounds, Driver heard "And are you acting?"

Driver said nothing.

"Because from here it starts to look like you're hanging back. You remember when we first talked about this? I asked what it was you wanted."

"Yes."

"Same thing then. If you don't want to carry through, you can go away again. Be missing."

Manny waited, then said: "Grand ideas is what we're taught. That mankind moves forward by grand ideas. You get older, you understand that nations aren't formed or wars fought for grand ideas, they happen because people don't want things to change."

The thwack-thwack of a helicopter came over the line. Sounded like a weed cutter one yard over.

"Think about it. I gotta go in and make nice for the money man, do the greasy smile and all—there's your creativity. Maybe we'll discuss how in the last twenty years the top one percent of Americans saw their share of the nation's wealth double while their tax burden shrank by a third. Or not. Talk to you soon."

At the time, both of them believed that.

The treatment Manny sketched out that day for the producer as barometric Scotch fell to the knothole and well below, riffing and spinning the story from whole cloth as he spoke, was about a man who drove, that was all he did, and about how he came to his end early one morning in a Tijuana bar. A hero for our time, the last frontiersman, Manny said. He almost said "a man exempt" but thought that would confuse things. And while the producer wrote him a check on the spot, the movie, like so many others, never got made.

Years later, blurry-eyed and clang-headed one intolerably bright morning, Manny found his draft of the script, which he'd long forgotten. By early afternoon he had a revision. By midnight he had it with his agent at APA.

"It is good to see you again. You've given what I said due consideration?"

Radically unlike the last time, the restaurant was at capacity, tables moved in close together to accommodate. Driver thought of New York, how you couldn't get up without jostling the neighbor's table. Back here, of course, there was space.

"A single malt, perhaps? An espresso? Are you hungry?"

"Nothing, thank you."

"Nothing. Yet you are here."

Beil looked toward the doors and immediately a server appeared. "Would you bring a small antipasto plate please, Mauro? And a glass of my Pinot Noir?"

The antipasto appeared within moments, as though lurking in the wings awaiting its turn onstage. Perhaps, but Driver found it hard to think of Beil as being that predictable. A separate server brought the wine. Crystal glass, silver tray, linen napkin.

"I came for a name."

"I see." Beil chewed at an olive, swallowed. "An agreement is in place?"

"For the moment."

"Ah. Then we have what politicians, ever wary of pinning themselves too close to the rose, might call a binding resolution." He sipped wine. "Surely you have a name by now."

"I know who's sitting across the board. Not the other players."

"The one you know is not only out of the picture—"

"For the moment."

"—he is also of no interest to me. To anyone, actually." Beil selected a divot of salami, then a chunk of ancient parmesan that looked like yellow stone. "You're certain you'll not have a drink?"

Driver nodded.

"Those you seek are wolves. Wolves do not wish to be found, they are themselves the hunters, slipping between trees, out of eyesight, close to the ground. They survive, they thrive, on their cunning." Beil bit off half an olive, peering into the hollow that was left. "They have been at their trade for hundreds of years. This way of life, it is in their blood, their bones."

"Their amygdyla."

Beil looked at him oddly. "Yes."

"And if I were looking for the big wolf, where would I go?"

"That wolf's name is Benjamin Capel. And you would go to a restaurant much like this one, though with appointments more...not of the gilt-statue-and-red-flocked-wallpaper variety, but close enough in spirit?"

Beil pushed an elegant business card across the table. Engraved, burnished silver characters, only the name, telephone number, and web address. Harlow's.

"This would be a good time for you to go calling, as it happens."

Driver stood.

"You might choose to make entry via the kitchen. A small, wiry man with a nose like a white potato and jet-black hair will be eating there. He's the gate you have to go through. Please do as little damage as possible?"

Driver looked back.

"The restaurant is half mine."

Two nights before they ripped out his throat, Benny Capel had talked to his wife about all the things he'd never do again.

She'd made a fine risotta with Parma ham and Parmesan, served it with a salad of mixed greens, apples, and walnuts. Afterwards they sat around out on the patio with a bottle of wine talking. Still hot, but with a breeze now and then, and a bright near-full moon. An owl sat in the pecan tree at the edge of the lawn. They could hear faint music from the neighbor's house beyond that and across the alley, light classical, soft jazz, something like that.

Nothing to eat after noon tomorrow, and all kinds of things to swallow. Cleaning out the pipes.

A pair of coyotes started up the drive, saw them, and turned back into the street.

"I'll never sing," he said.

"You never did."

"And I'll never be able to shout when I get angry."

"You don't get angry. Not so anyone can see."

"I'll never spend hours on the phone talking to friends, never talk back to the television, hum along with the radio. Never whisper in your ear. And I'll never laugh."

Janis just looked at him then and said, "I'll be your laughter."

They didn't laugh much anymore, either of them, but he remembered her saying that, and how she looked when she said it, and how he felt.

He'd never forget that.

The discussion in the kitchen had run about two minutes. Even out here, you could smell burned flesh. Nonetheless, Capel kept looking that way.

"Your man's in the walk-in freezer," Driver said. "Cooling off."

A waiter stepped up to a table with two plates of food only to realize that his diners had jumped ship. Customers were quick-stepping away from others. Three over, by the wall, Driver watched a man turn in his chair and pull back his sport coat. Carrying, no doubt.

"This is personal," Driver said. "I'm not armed." The man nodded.

Capel looked up. He was older than expected, late sixties, early seventies, wearing a robin's-egg-blue shirt, darker blue tie, and black suit shot with silver pinstripes that matched his hair. He held both hands out to show they were empty, then reached for a small cylinder on the table by his plate. That was silver too. Held it to his throat. The voice that came out was surprisingly warm and inflected. "You would be the driver."

Driver didn't respond.

"Did you come to kill me?"

Again, Driver said nothing.

"And with your bare hands." Capel looked around. "But of course there are knives, aren't there? Dangerous objects everywhere." He pointed. "And that man's gun. A Glock—the new favorite of the feds. My wife says they keep investigating me only because it allows them to eat well."

"Maybe we should talk outside. Before *all* your customers leave."

Capel came to his feet easily, a man who kept himself in shape. He plucked a breadstick from the tumbler filled with them. Electrolarynx in one hand, breadstick in the other. "To defend myself."

They walked outside, where two cars, a gleaming black BMW and a kickass old Buick, were pulling away. The restaurant sat on a dogleg off major streets, so there was little traffic. Up toward Goldwater a restaurant's outside patio was choked with young people, misters going full-out. From here, it sounded like flocks of birds. And it looked as though the birds were washing down, drink after drink, food that hadn't happened yet.

"You, this thing with you, that's business too, you know," Capel said.

"Look at it a certain way, everything's business. The simplest conversation becomes an economic exchange."

"Yes. Both sides want something." Capel took the cylinder away for a moment, as though on a microphone and clearing his throat. "True, too, that generally the desired ends are not so transparent. You want your life, and me out of it. As of but minutes ago, I would like the same."

A black Escalade eased along the street and into the lot. A tall, thin man, pale with feathery white hair, climbed out.

"They'll have called, from inside." Capel's hand lifted, made a slight push at the air. The man leaned back against the van, watching.

"It's no easy thing," Capel said, "but I can call this off. I have the weight to do that. But it won't be over."

"I understand."

"I'm sure you do. Neither, then, are our negotiations."

"No."

"You're an unpopular man. Memorable—but remarkably unpopular. You have no friends, for instance, in Brooklyn. Around Henry Street, say, where old women sit on the stoops in their aprons and men play dominoes on cardtables by the curb."

Capel looked past him. "These would be yours." Driver turned. A gray Chevrolet sedan coming in slow. Two heads. "The PPD, subtle as ever. Completely anonymous in their unmarked car."

The driver's door opened and a man got out who looked like an accountant. Room for half of another neck in his shirt collar, bad tie, wayward elbows and knees.

Billie's father got out on the other side.

"What you described, how things were getting handled, it had to come back to Bennie. No one else locally has the machinery, the people in place. Figured I'd swing by, talk to him about it. The two of us go back some years."

"When you were a cop."

"Before that."

Bill's companion was Nate Sanderson, who Bill said had done time in the FBI, then in the DA's office, before settling in with the department, and had now gone too lazy to move again. Not to mention the excellent pay and job security, of course.

"You found out what you needed?" Sanderson asked.

"Hell if I know." It was turning into one of those situations, Driver thought, where every answer you get confuses you more. To Bill he said, "Aren't you missing Andy Griffith back at the home?"

"I'll catch up next time."

"What, you escaped?"

"Man walks in, flashes a badge, they're not likely to ask a lot of questions. One reason I needed Nate here."

"The other?"

"He works organized crime. Squeezing the rag. Knows where to find Bennie this time of day."

They were in a cavernous, mostly empty restaurant off Missouri. The handpainted sign out front read only *Chicken Ribs*, with a primitive cartoon of a fox licking its lips. Those would be some mighty small ribs, Bill had said. He and Sanderson were eating slices of pie that looked to be about 80 percent meringue. Driver had coffee. He watched as a light-skinned man passed on the sidewalk wearing a t-shirt with *We Are All Illegal Aliens* in bold capitals front and back.

"I can't seem to find a straight line anywhere in this," Driver said.

Bill glanced out the window to see what he was watching. "Nature's never been big on straight lines."

"Or people," Sanderson said.

Driver had assumed that once he had the handle, once he made his way to Capel, everything would tumble right back onto the guy in New Orleans, Dunaway. But it didn't. The road curved, and you couldn't see around the bend. Capel didn't know Dunaway from hot mustard. Word came down, he said, "from one of the motherships," and when Driver asked where the ship was harbored, he said Brooklyn.

Dunaway was from Brooklyn. Old connections? Or just work for hire?

Bill shook his head. "Conceivably they'd lend their guys, but they don't hire out."

"Calling in old markers, then?"

"Or favors. Borrow your tool for the day? Could be."

Came in as a simple take-down, Capel had said. But then when he passed word up the line, he was told the situation had changed, he was to keep his men out there.

"What changed?" Sanderson said.

They sat quietly. Finally Bill spoke. "They have history with our friend here."

Both looked at Driver. He nodded.

"A long time back. A man named Nino, big up that way. And his right-hand man." Bernie Rose.

"You killed them?"

"Yes."

"These guys don't have short memories." Bill peered out the window. An elderly man who looked like a weathered piece of rope had pulled his bicycle into the crosswalk, slammed down the kickstand, and walked away. He stood on the corner watching as one car, trying to avoid running into it, slewed into another.

"People will do anything to make their mark," Sanderson said.

"Maybe just to prove to themselves that they're alive." Bill looked back. "But Bennie told you he sent word up the line. Never mind how the job came about.

Source, Channels. Bennie sent word, it means that as far as he knew the job was done."

"But it wasn't. I walked away."

"Right."

"That doesn't make sense," Sanderson said.

"Not the kind of sense you've been trying to make," Bill said to Driver. "You can't find a straight line because there isn't one. There's more than one and they don't meet. They're parallel."

Cruising away cross-city, Camelback in his rear-view mirror, Driver saw a billboard, one of those horrendous new digital ones that changed every few minutes. JESUS DIED FOR YOUR SINS, it said, above a stylized figure that could be rabbi, priest, or big-hair preacher, hand raised in supplication. That went away to be supplanted by the close-up of a man who had the look of running-for-office about him. Probably born with the look, but he'd worked on it some. Wide face, sincere eyes, hair perfectly parted. DON'T MAKE A MOVE TILL YOU TALK TO US, the legend read. Sims and Barrow, Attorneys at Law.

Driver laughed.

Shannon would have loved it.

Minutes ago, he was thinking about Bernie Rose. Now Shannon. Thinking about how almost everyone he knew was gone.

About Elsa.

That smile she got when he said or did something really dumb. Her voice beside him in the night. The drowned-dog look of her hair as she stepped out of the shower and the way she looked that last day, propped against the wall of the empty café, blood pumping from her chest.

The cell phone rang. Driver flipped it open.

Felix. "You know someone named Blanche?"

"No." Driver pulled up at a light behind an ancient van whose rear doors were covered with stickers. They'd been there so long that none of them were legible. Shapes and blurred patches of color. "Yes."

Blanche's shoulders lying across the bathroom door's threshhold, the pool of blood lapping toward him. Not much of her head left in there.

And he was back at the Motel 6 not far from here, standing again at the window thinking it had to be Blanche, no other way that Chevy was down there in the parking lot.

Then the shotgun blast.

Blanche and her accent, saying she was from New Orleans, sounding like Bensonhurst.

There it was: Brooklyn again.

"Blanche Davis," Felix said.

"Not the name she was using."

"Lady had a casual way with names. Blanche Dunlop, Carol Saint-Mars, Betty Ann Proulx. Pretty much a moving target, too. Dallas, St. Louis, Portland, Jersey City. Scams, hard hustles. Coupla hinky marriages in there. She got around."

"And what, her name just popped up?"

"Not quite. Doyle had to kind of stick his finger in there and pull. You know." Felix was quiet for a moment. "There's more."

"Okay."

"Your man Dunaway?"

Driver waited.

"He's in town."

"Where?"

"About four feet away from me. Want to come say hello?"

Driver had gone less than a mile before traffic slowed almost to a halt as one of Phoenix's epic dust storms rolled in. You felt it at the base of your throat, behind your eyelids, could barely make out the car in front of you, or road's edge and the banks beyond. Dust burrowed in like guilt or regret, you couldn't get away from it, couldn't get rid of it. And Driver couldn't get rid of thoughts of Bernie Rose. He sat in the landlocked car thinking about that last time, how Bernie had asked if he thought we choose our lives and he'd said no, what it felt like was, they're forever seeping up under us.

"You don't think we change?" Driver had asked as they walked out of the restaurant.

"Change? No. What we do is adapt. Get by. Time you're ten, twelve years old, it's pretty much set in you, what you're going to be like, what your life's going to be."

Moments before he had to put Bernie down.

So maybe Bernie was right.

Driver pulled into the parking lot just as the storm abated. People would be sneezing wee mudballs and wiping dirt out of every crease and crack in themselves, their houses, cars, and property for a week.

Not a Motel 6, but its kissing cousin. Spiderwebbed asphalt patched with tar, roof drooping above the second-floor walkway, blinds cockeyed in windows. Three cars in the lot, two of them questionably mobile. A café and bar sat to other side, back a bit. Take a brave man to hit that café, but Driver guessed the bar did good business. Run-down apartments all around, bus stop across the street.

Room 109 was at the end, abutting a slump block wall with grout that looked like poorly healed scars and, past that, an abandoned convenience store, every possible surface scribbled over with tags.

Guy has money to burn, he winds up here? Driver thought.

But not his idea, most likely.

Slats in the blinds fell back into place as Driver approached. Felix opened the door without speaking.

Inside, a man in his late sixties sat watching CNN, a news report about upcoming democratic elections somewhere halfway across the world. Driver tried to remember the last time he'd seen a seersucker suit. The man was sipping whiskey from a plastic cup, not cheap stuff from the smell of it. So was Felix.

"Doyle." Felix nodded toward the corner. Doyle had light blue eyes, an expression that could be a wide smile or pain. Looked younger than Driver knew he must be. Mom's favorite, a good all-American boy.

Doyle nodded.

The older man glanced away from the TV. "You're the driver." Then to Doyle: "He doesn't look quite dead."

"No sir. I suppose I did stretch the truth just a little."

Felix poured more for himself, then for the man in the chair. "Doyle persuaded Mr. Dunaway, by way of an anonymous phone call, that those pursuing you had finally been successful, and that you'd left behind something in which he might well be interested. 'Something to do with Blanche?' Mr. Dunaway asked.

"Doyle followed him, picked him up here at Sky Harbor. Too many walls and fences back in New Orleans, the need was to get him away."

"And out here to the golden west," Doyle said. "He came along without protest. At the airport."

The man said, "Rabbits that survive know when to go to ground."

Driver moved around to meet his eyes. "You're a rabbit, Mr. Dunaway?"

"A survivor. And surrounded by foxes. Like him." Dunaway pointed to the TV. Driver turned to look. An elderly man with his arms in the air, circled by others, all young, wearing rags and tatters of uniforms and carrying automatic weapons. "Strange missions. We're all chockful of strange missions. Often we don't even know what they are. But they push us, they ride us."

"You're saying you didn't choose to pursue me?"

"Not at all. That was one thing I understood. But the rest…"

"Who was Blanche, sir?"

"Only a sweet, troubled girl. They're everywhere. All around us."

He said nothing more. They listened to a car pull into the lot outside, sit with speakers blasting, and pull away.

"Why are you trying to kill me, Mr. Dunaway?"

The screen showed hundreds of birds rising from a lake. It was as though the surface of the lake itself were drifting skyward. Dunaway glanced there, then back.

"Kill you? Not at all. Quite the contrary."

He finished his Scotch and set the cup on the floor.

"The story's not much different from what you hear from parents everywhere, We did what we could. We could see her getting wilder every year, every day. Small things at first, stealing from friends, shoplifting, then gone for days at a time. One night she's passed out in bed with all her clothes on and I'm looking in her purse hoping I won't find drugs, and I don't. I find a gun. Not long after that, she was gone for good."

"Blanche was your daughter."

Dunaway nodded. "We knew she was bad, just a lost person, hurtful, destructive. But that made no difference."

"I'm sorry."

"You were with her."

"When she was killed. Yes sir, I was."

"Wasn't likely to play out any other way. Her life."

"No."

"We did what we could. Once my wife was gone…" Dunaway broke off eye contact to look back at the screen. "Blanche was my only child. You took her from me."

"No sir, the man who did that died moments after she did."

"I'd been searching for her. One of the private detectives I hired came to my house to tell me he'd found her. Bubble of hope, for a moment there. I remember he was wearing jeans—pressed jeans with a sport coat. And a shiny shirt, like satin. Blanche had died two weeks before."

No one said anything. Doyle watched the door and window, Felix watched the old man. Felix had no expression on his face. Dunaway's sadness filled the room like an unseen gas.

"I wasn't trying to kill you, young man. Quite the contrary. I wanted you alive, to go on feeling what it's like to have the person most important to you taken away, to carry that around for the rest of your life."

"Elsa? Those two men came for Elsa, not for me?"

"That was the plan. I don't think they realized who, or what, you are. Few apparently do. And the plan…"

All became quiet again. Two or three rooms away, a telephone rang.

"Never mind the plan," Dunaway said. "Things got complicated, the way things do. Might I have one last drink? I assume you brought me here to kill me."

Felix poured and the old man drank. Onscreen, cameras panned across acre after acre of drifting dunes.

"Understand," Dunaway said, "that this would come as a great relief."

"He's back in New Orleans." Where, in a moment of strangeness Doyle had said, the magnolia blossoms smell like sweet human flesh.

"Cruelty or compassion?" Bill asked.

Driver shrugged.

Bill and Nate Sanderson had met him at a Filiberto's on Indian School, and now they were walking along the canal, dodging crazed bikers and dogwalkers as evening settled about them. Bill was playing hooky again.

"So that part is over," Bill said.

"For some time, really."

"The world's never what we think it is."

They stopped to look down into the canal: three shopping carts had been neatly stacked like auditorium chairs, a worn blanket rolled, tied with strings into a facsimile human, and set atop them. Water flowed through the carts, up to the blanketman's bent knees.

"Beautify your city," Bill said. Then, "Nate and I had another talk with Bennie Capel. But this time at home, with his wife there. Bennie at home's not the Bennie you see elsewhere. Janis and I go back a ways too."

It took him a while, and it wasn't in the neighborhood of smooth, but Bill stepped off the path and sat
on the graveled side of the canal, legs down along the
curve of the bank. Driver sat beside him. They looked
back at Sanderson, who shook his head. "Bad knees."

"It was a favor among old friends, from Dunaway's
life back in Brooklyn. A simple take-down, they're in,
they're done, they're out. But when it didn't go that way,
the bigger fish had to wonder what the hell happened.
They dispatch two of their wing men and some guy in
Bumfuck, Arizona wiped the street with them? That
does not *happen*."

"It was Elsa they were sent after."

"Up to that point, yeah. But then the eyes go to you.
They talk to Dunaway, they talk to his detectives, his
informants. They get answers. And finally they make
the connection. This Nino, and Bernie Rose. Two
more of theirs, and from a long time back, but they got
memories. Dunaway's out of the picture now. Blood's
coming up in *their* eyes."

"You do make an impression," Sanderson said.

"I have Bennie's word." Bill picked up a piece of
gravel and tossed it in. "His people won't touch you.
Doesn't mean that when the plane from the east coast
lands there won't be others getting off it."

"That much, I'd figured out." Driver watched as an
athletic shoe rafted lazily down the canal. For a moment

he thought he saw a face peering out, a rat, a hamster. "You're making this a habit, going over the wall."

"Well…seems I've had my fill of spaghetti and jello. This time, I won't be going back."

"Good plan. What'll you do?"

"Who knows? Play it by ear, see where life leads, I guess."

"Still a good plan. And your friend Wendell? What's he going to do without you?"

"Oh, I suspect we'll be getting together for coffee. Maybe a night on the town, though at our age it'll be a short night. And I suspect he won't be long finding someone else to badger."

"It's been good getting to know you, Bill. Walking beside you."

"Right back at you, young man. One thing?"

"Yes, sir."

"Go by and see my girl?"

Driver had tucked the Fairlane away on the middle level of a three-tier parking garage by an office building populated chiefly by doctors of the asthma, spinal injury, and cardiac sort. Lots of repeat business, lots of comings and goings, easy access and exit. As he emerged from the bare-bones stairwell, cement and featureless gray paint, a figure stepped from the shadow by his car.

"I thought I might come to you, this last time," Beil said. "To thank you for your assistance. And to give you this."

A business card embossed with only a phone number.

"Should you ever find yourself…at a total loss, let us say…call that number."

Driver held up the card. "I did nothing to help you."

"Ah, but you did, even if you are unable to see it. We so rarely understand what effects our actions have. Or will have. *We in some strange power's employ.*"

A Ford F-150 swung up the ramp and too fast around the curve, braking just inches behind a Buick backing out. The Buick's elderly driver also hit his brakes, and sat unmoving. The pickup's horn blew.

"You're a strange power?" Driver said.

"Not at all. Only one of many, indeed most, caught in between. Like you." Beil stepped closer. "Ride lightly, as your friend Felix would say, and with an eye always to the mirror. Bennie's tigers will not harm you. About the others, we can do nothing. For now."

Driver nodded.

"And so, again," Beil said, "you disappear. Though—" He held up a closed fist, turned it palm upward, opened it—"is that not, deep within yourself, down where the blind fish live, perhaps what you wanted all along?"

The pickup pulled into the space left vacant by the Buick. Its door opened, and first one crutch, then another, emerged. The driver hopped down between them, wearing yellow and purple running shoes.

Beil turned back. "My wife suffers from dementia. Nothing filigree and trendy such as Alzheimer's, mind you, but plain old dementia. Each morning as I leave I go to kiss her and she tells me, I love you like butter, every morning for eleven, twelve years. This morning what she said, with no notion that something was wrong, something was different, was: I love you like rubber. Take the lesson from my wife. Love your life like butter. Like rubber."

Driver walked to the edge and moments later watched Beil come out of the stairwell. Two black sedans pulled up immediately at curbside.

He got out of the Fairlane, walked around to the front of the garage. She straightened and leaned to look past the open hood of a '57 Chevy Bel Air. The clamp floodlight on her bench was on. With the light behind her, he couldn't see her face.

"You've come to say good-bye."

Driver nodded.

"I saw you back there. Then you waited." She reached behind to snap off the light, stepped to the car's side. "Never gets easy, does it?"

"I've had practice."

"You have, but I don't mean saying good-bye. Making choices."

She popped the top of the cooler under her bench, handed him a beer, got one herself.

"Our eyes bounce off surfaces, we can't see far or deep. We make choices from the pitifully little we understand about who we are, held in place by that. Then we hold our breaths fully expecting the heavens to tear open at any minute. All of us do that, Eight. Not just you."

Again he thought about Bernie, *Time you're ten, twelve years old, it's pretty much set in you, what you're going to be like, what your life's going to be.*

"Comforting," he said.

"It is, in a way. Like this." Billie held up her beer. "It's all a storm, Eight. But we have these bright days, these calms."

"You were one."

She laughed. "You bet your ass I was. Now get out of here, I've got work to do—once I undo what all the heads that have been under this hood before did to the poor girl."

They picked him up just outside Mesa, a Chrysler and a BMW. He cut off and back onto I-10, jumped an exit and feeder road to head back toward Phoenix, then clipped off again and on toward Tucson. Feared for a while that he might have lost them and pulled over. Sat at roadside, the Indian casino's electronic billboard flashing against his windshield, semis whipping by, waiting. Till there they were. When the two cars drew within easy distance he peeled out ahead, braked and wheeled his way into a 180, drove behind and spun again, came up behind them and shot past.

In the rearview mirror he watched them moving toward him. He turned the radio on. He smiled.

He drove.

To receive a free catalog of Poisoned Pen Press titles, please contact us in one of the following ways:

Phone: 1-800-421-3976
Facsimile: 1-480-949-1707
Email: info@poisonedpenpress.com
Website: www.poisonedpenpress.com

Poisoned Pen Press
6962 E. First Ave. Ste 103
Scottsdale, AZ 85251